Fatherhood Unplugged

A Guide to Parenting Through Pain Without Passing It On

Book Cover by Daniel McMahon
Illustrations by Daniel McMahon
Self-Published by: Daniel McMahon
1st edition 2025
ISBN: 978-1-7640288-7-5

Copyright©2025 By Daniel McMahon

DEDICATION

This book is here for all parents navigating the beautiful yet complex journey of Fatherhood Unplugged: A Guide to Parenting Through Pain Without Passing It On.

Your incredible strength and resilience shine brightly, acknowledging the mothers, fathers, grandparents, and caregivers who work tirelessly to create a stable, loving environment for their children, even in the most challenging times. I want to express my heartfelt gratitude to my two loving foster children, who have shown me more about love, patience, and perseverance than I ever thought possible. This journey indeed came to life because of you.

You are never alone in every family that has faced challenges, but you continue choosing love, understanding, and growth. May this book serve as a beacon of hope, guiding you toward smoother waters and reminding you that family is always at the heart of transformation.

With all my love and admiration,
Daniel McMahon

TABLE OF CONTENTS

INTRODUCTION

It was one of those days. You know, the kind where everything seems to pile up like a never-ending mountain of laundry. I stood in the kitchen, surrounded by the chaos of breakfast dishes and half-packed lunchboxes. My two kids were at the table, arguing over something trivial, as kids do. And then it happened—I heard my father's voice coming out of my mouth. I was yelling, really yelling. The yelling that leaves a mark, the kind I promised myself I'd never do.

I stopped mid-sentence. It was like time froze for a moment. The look in their eyes mirrored the one I used to have, that mix of fear and confusion. That was the moment I knew everything had to change. I didn't want to pass on the pain of my upbringing. I wanted something better for my kids and myself.

This book is about that change. It's about transforming fatherhood into a journey of healing and growth. We can break the cycle and stop passing down burdens that aren't ours to give. Fatherhood doesn't have to be about repeating the past. It can be about creating a different, healthier, and more fulfilling future.

Let me tell you who I am. I'm a single dad, and I've been married twice. My first marriage was to someone beautiful and kind, and I'll be honest—if I had access to what I know now, I would've been a better man and partner. I didn't have the tools back then. I was still locked in survival mode, pretending I was fine while quietly unraveling.

My second marriage was different. It was with someone battling severe mental illness, and I didn't know how to manage her pain, my pain, or the pressure of holding everything together. I was running to work, racing home, looking after the kids, navigating emotional minefields, and still pretending to have it all under control. But the truth is, I had no idea how to feel my feelings, let alone teach my kids how to manage theirs.

Today, I'm in EMDR therapy. I'm going back to my childhood— painful as it is—to finally start healing the things I was told to "get over." That process has been brutal, beautiful, and necessary. And it's what inspired this book. Not just therapy, but the research helped. The healing helped. But what changed everything was the decision to stop pretending and start parenting from a place of honesty.

This book isn't written from a psychologist's chair. It's written from the kitchen table, the car's front seat at school pickup, and the quiet of a kid-free night when you're just trying to catch your breath. It's a real dad's guide to healing while parenting—and messing up—and doing better the next time.

So why this book? Because I know I'm not alone. Some fathers are tired of the old ways and want to build something better for their families. This book is for you. It's for those seeking to break negative cycles and foster healthier family dynamics. Emotional healing and personal growth are not just buzzwords—they're the foundation for a better relationship with our children and ourselves.

What can you expect? We'll explore themes like emotional resilience and communication strategies. We'll discuss breaking generational cycles and what it means to parent with awareness and intention. I'll share my missteps, the times I stumbled, and the lessons I learned. These stories and insights will offer you something valuable for your journey.

CHAPTER 1

AWAKENING TO A NEW FATHERHOOD

I was sitting at the kitchen table, surrounded by the usual morning chaos. Cereal spilled across the counter, kids were arguing, and a to-do list seemed to grow by the minute. As I tried to referee the squabble, I heard it—a familiar voice booming, echoing around the room like a bad rerun of my childhood. It wasn't just any voice. It was the voice of authority from my past that brooked no opposition and left little room for discussion. My kids stopped mid-bicker, eyes wide, and it hit me like a freight train. I was repeating the very patterns I had vowed to leave behind. It was as if my father's ghost had slipped into my skin, and I was channeling him through my vocal cords. At that moment, a childhood memory resurfaced. I remembered feeling small and scared as my father's voice thundered around me. The fear was tangible, and I could see that same fear mirrored in my children's eyes. This moment—this jarring, eye-opening realization—was my catalyst for change. It became clear that what I had inherited wasn't working. The urgency to break free from these chains and create a healthier dynamic for my children was undeniable.

The Moment I Knew I Didn't Want to Parent Like I Was Raised

Growing up, my world was painted with broad strokes of authoritarian colors, little room for error, and love that often felt conditional. The communication style was more commanding than conversational. If you didn't toe the line, you faced the consequences. My dad wasn't an evil man; he was doing his best with the tools he had. But his toolbox was filled with wrenches and hammers when we needed paintbrushes and palettes. Contrast that with what I wanted for my family now—a home where empathy leads the way, where communication is an open dialogue rather than a series of directives. I craved a space where love didn't have strings attached, where support was unconditional, not contingent on achievements or behavior. You see, authoritarian parenting can lead to compliance out of fear, but it doesn't foster trust or emotional connection. Empathetic communication is about understanding and validating feelings before moving to solutions.

It's about listening as much as—or more than—you speak. Realizing this need for change hit me hard emotionally. My initial feelings were a cocktail of anxiety and shame mixed with a dash of fear. What if I couldn't be different? What if the patterns were too ingrained? Anxiety whispered that I might repeat those mistakes. Shame shouted that maybe I wasn't good enough to break free. Those feelings crept up uninvited, making themselves comfortable in my psyche. But there's power in recognizing these emotions, facing them head-on, and refusing to let them dictate your actions. My commitment to change didn't come with a grand declaration or a Hollywood-style transformation montage. It was more subtle—a decision made in quiet moments when the kids were asleep, and the house was still. I realized I needed personal parenting goals that focused on building a new framework for our family dynamic.

I sought resources and read everything about conscious parenting and emotional intelligence. Support groups became lifelines where I found friendship and shared experiences that bolstered my resolve. The commitment to fostering a healthier family dynamic wasn't just lip service; it became a daily practice, an ongoing project with no set deadline but plenty of milestones to celebrate. Through this process, I learned that change doesn't happen overnight. It's not a switch you flip but a gradual shift in perspective and behavior. Setting personal parenting goals helped me focus on the big picture while navigating the day-to-day challenges. From seeking advice through parenting workshops to conversing with other dads facing similar battles, every step was about building something new and enduring. This journey isn't always easy, but it's worth it. When you see your child's eyes reflecting trust instead of fear or when they come to you with their worries, knowing they'll be met with understanding rather than judgment—that's when you know it's working. That's when you realize that breaking away from inherited patterns isn't just possible—it's powerful. As we navigate this path together, remember that change doesn't demand perfection; it asks only for progress and intention. It asks us to show up daily, willing to learn, grow, and love fiercely. Let's embrace this new fatherhood with open hearts and minds, ready to rewrite our stories and create ones our children will cherish.

Meet the Inner Chaos Crew: Anxiety, Shame, and the Critic

Let me introduce you to a cast of characters that are all too familiar in the theater of daily life: anxiety, shame, and the ever-present critic. These three mischievous entities seem to have set up residence on my shoulder, constantly whispering doubts and tossing obstacles into my path when all I'm trying to do is make it through the day. Don't mistake them for imaginary companions; they are emotional saboteurs, lurking behind every corner, gearing up to strike at any parental misstep or perceived error. Anxiety, for instance, behaves much like an overzealous bodyguard, forged in the crucible of past traumas and always standing ready and hyper-vigilant. It warns me to be cautious, suggesting that every decision carries the potential weight of impending disaster. Then there's the critic, that relentless voice questioning every parental choice I make. Is that the best you're capable of? Didn't you botch that? And let us not forget shame, the stealthiest of them all, infusing the air with painful reminders of unmet needs from the past, perpetuating the belief that I'll never be quite enough. These voices can transform the simplest parenting decision into a treacherous minefield. Gaining insight into the origins of these emotions is akin to peeling away the layers of an onion, often bringing tears to the surface. Anxiety frequently finds its roots in a childhood filled with unyielding parental expectations, ones that were seemingly etched in stone. This breeds a constant fear of falling short, of not measuring up, as anything less than perfect is considered unacceptable.

On the other hand, shame can often be traced back to an upbringing where validation was as scarce as a rare gem. Growing up feeling unseen or undervalued makes it all too easy to carry forward a belief into adulthood that one is inherently flawed or undeserving of honors. Yet, there lies a silver lining: merely because these emotions have a longstanding presence does not mean they are allowed to steer the ship. Recognizing when they begin to dominate is the initial step toward reclaiming control. Mindfulness exercises come into play here. They serve as mental spotlights, illuminating those sneaky, stealthy emotions before they have an opportunity to cause chaos. Sitting with one's thoughts and observing them without judgment can make a profound difference. And let's not overlook journaling—a tool that, though simple, holds immense power. It's akin to dialogue with oneself, truly exploring feelings and unveiling what lies beneath the surface layers.

Reflection Exercise

Allocate a few moments each day to jot down any feelings of anxiety or shame that arise. Document what incites them and how they manifest in your thoughts, behaviors, and actions. This practice aids in uncovering patterns and understanding the deep-seated roots of these emotions. Building a constructive and positive relationship with your feelings isn't about ignoring or pretending they aren't there; it's about reframing them as signposts rather than roadblocks. Anxiety needn't be an adversary; it can become an opportunity for self-examination, a chance to consider what genuinely matters and understand why specific situations provoke such robust responses. The inner critic doesn't need to be silenced entirely; instead, it can be transformed into a guide for self-improvement. Picture it as having an internal editor who can help hone your parenting narrative without dismantling the entire story. Shame is perhaps the most complex and indefinable of all. It flourishes in secrecy but withers under the bright light of understanding and empathy. By acknowledging its presence and delving into its origins, you can begin to dismantle its hold. It's about permitting yourself to be less than perfect, to err without allowing mistakes to define your worth as a parent or individual. These emotions are fundamentally human; they don't vanish overnight, yet they don't have to derail your parenting efforts either. Recognizing and managing them creates a space ripe for growth and healing for yourself and your children. They are allowed to witness a parent who embodies reality and vulnerability, who acknowledges personal struggles but refuses to allow them to impede love and connection. It's about approaching each day with an open heart, prepared to tackle whatever unfolds with honesty and courage. That's the kind of parent I aspire to be— not perfect, but present; not infallible, but willing to learn and evolve alongside my kids. And perhaps that's the essence of what truly matters in the end: not that we have all the answers, but that we remain poised to ask the right questions and keep moving forward together. So here's to greeting our inner chaos crew with empathy and understanding—listening to their concerns without letting them preside over our choices—and creating a life that acknowledges and embraces all the messy, beautiful complexities of the human experience.

Yelling Was My Default Language—Until I Heard Myself

The day I realized yelling had become my go-to parenting tool was ordinary. Yet, as is often the case, the profound shifts usually hide within the mundane. I was in the living room, refereeing a squabble over a crayon set between my two kids. Their voices were raised, and in a split second, so was mine. The words flew out, sharp and unyielding, slicing through the air with an unexpected force. It was one of those out-of-body experiences where you hear yourself and wonder if that's your voice. My words echoed back, and I saw my children's faces change. Their eyes widened, not from understanding but from shock—and maybe a bit of fear. It was a jolt to my system. Suddenly, I was on the receiving end of my actions, and the impact hit me harder than I'd anticipated. Observing their reactions was like looking into a mirror reflecting my childhood experiences. Their flinch reminded me of how yelling had often been used to communicate when I was growing up. It was a tool that seemed effective in the short term but left emotional scars that lingered far longer. Realizing that I might be repeating this cycle was more than unsettling; it was downright terrifying. As I sat with this newfound awareness, I began to explore the triggers behind my inclination to raise my voice. Stress played a significant role. Balancing work demands with family life often left me feeling stretched thin, like too little butter over too much bread. The weight of responsibility felt immense, and yelling was an easy release valve when tensions ran high. But it wasn't just stress; it was also a learned behavior inherited from the communication patterns I grew up with. The idea that volume equaled authority had been etched into my psyche long ago. Recognizing these triggers was only part of the solution.

The real work lies in implementing change. I needed new strategies and healthier communication methods that didn't involve raising my voice. One simple yet effective tactic I found was taking a time-out, not for the kids, but for myself. When I felt the urge to yell bubbling up, I'd step away for a moment to cool down. It wasn't always easy, but it made a difference in how I responded. Practicing active listening became another cornerstone of change. Instead of reacting impulsively, I began to truly listen to what my kids were saying. This shift helped me engage more empathetically with my children during conflicts. Incorporating empathy into our conversations was transformative, too.

I learned to approach their concerns with kindness rather than criticism by trying to see things from their perspective. This not only improved our communication but also strengthened our relationship. When they felt heard and understood, they were more open to dialogue and less likely to respond defiantly. Celebrating progress became a vital part of this journey. Change doesn't happen overnight, and acknowledging small victories kept me motivated. Keeping a journal of successful interactions helped reinforce new habits. Whenever I handled a situation without raising my voice, I'd jot it down as a reminder that positive change was possible. Setting personal milestones for communication improvement gave me tangible goals to work towards. Each time I reached one, it was a cause for celebration—a step forward to becoming the parent I aspired to be. Let's briefly talk about journaling—a potent tool for tracking growth and development. It's more than just writing down events; it's about reflecting on experiences, understanding patterns, and setting intentions for future interactions. By documenting those moments where I managed to hold back from yelling, I created a record of progress that kept me accountable.

As you embark on your path towards healthier communication (pun intended), remember to celebrate each success, no matter how small it may seem. Change isn't about perfection; it's about progress. Recognize your efforts and give yourself grace when you stumble. Raising kids is no small feat; it's a marathon, not a sprint. While yelling might feel like an easy shortcut in the heat of the moment, its long-term effects can be damaging. We break the cycle and build stronger connections with our children by choosing healthier communication methods. Through this process, you'll find that your home becomes more peaceful, where understanding reigns over anger, and love is communicated clearly and calmly. Embrace each step along this path with patience and compassion for yourself and those around you. In closing—or instead, without closing—let's remember that every effort towards better communication is worth it. The rewards are immeasurable: healthier relationships with our children, improved emotional well-being for ourselves, and an environment where everyone feels valued and heard.

Unlearning Love That Hurt: Affection Without Fear.

Redefining love isn't as simple as flipping a switch or turning a page. It's more like gently untangling a ball of yarn that's been knotted up for years. Growing up, I often confused love with anxiety. I thought that if I worried enough about someone, it meant I loved them more. This love-as-anxiety notion was like a shadow, creeping into my relationships and parenting. It was protective, yes, but it was also suffocating. It took me time to realize that real love isn't about control or fear. It's about freedom and respect. Love shouldn't feel like a tightrope walk where one misstep leads to disaster. Instead, it should be a soft place to land, where safety and acceptance are the norms. As a kid, conditional love seemed like the norm. Achievements were celebrated; failures were quietly ignored or met with disappointment. Unknowingly, I internalized that love had to be earned and came with strings attached.

When I became a parent, I noticed traces of this conditional affection slipping into my interactions with my children. It was an uncomfortable realization that pushed me to redefine what love and affection should look like in our home. Creating safe affection begins with respect—respect for boundaries and individuality. Physical affection should be warm, not overwhelming. Hugging your child when they are receptive to it, rather than forcing it upon them, is key. It's about understanding that their comfort matters. When upset, my kids sometimes need a hand on their shoulder or a gentle acknowledgment of their feelings. It's amazing how these small gestures can convey love without words. Verbal affirmations play a significant role, too. They're like little seeds planted in the minds of our children, reinforcing their self-worth and potential. Telling your child you're proud of them for who they are, not just what they do, is powerful. It builds a foundation of unconditional support they can lean on as they grow. Simple words of encouragement can make a difference, reminding them they are loved for simply existing. Healing from past hurts requires confronting the painful experiences that have shaped our understanding of love.

Therapy or counseling can be invaluable in this process. Sitting with a professional provides a safe space to explore these emotions and begin the healing journey. Talking through those old wounds helps to release their grip on our present lives. It's not about forgetting the past but understanding it enough to move forward without its weight. Reflective exercises also help identify triggers—those moments when past hurts rear their heads in present situations. Journaling can be therapeutic here. Writing down reactions and feelings when they arise allows us to recognize patterns and consciously try to change them. It's about being mindful of the old tapes playing in our heads and choosing to rewrite the script. Creating new narratives is about embracing the present and letting go of outdated beliefs.

Storytelling with children becomes an opportunity to instill values of unconditional love and acceptance. Sharing stories where kindness prevails over fear and support trumps judgment reinforces these values. It shows children that they are loved no matter what, setting them up for healthier relationships in their own lives. Family rituals can also celebrate emotional expression and strengthen the bonds between loved ones. Whether it's a weekly family dinner where everyone shares highs and lows or bedtime stories highlighting kindness and empathy, these traditions create an environment where love is openly expressed and cherished. Through these practices, we craft a family narrative that reflects our current values and beliefs rather than those inherited from the past. This narrative isn't static; it evolves as we do. It adapts to our family's needs, growing with us as we learn and change together. In this ongoing process of redefining love, we find healing, not just for ourselves but for our children as well.

We break free from patterns that no longer serve us and create spaces where affection is expressed without fear or control. The journey towards healthier expressions of love is one of growth and self-discovery. It requires patience and persistence, but brings immense rewards—the joy of watching your children thrive in an environment where they feel valued and secure. As we strive to unlearn love that hurts and embrace affection without fear, let us remember that each step forward is progress worth celebrating. Let us be kind to ourselves in this process, knowing that change takes time but creates a lasting impact. In reimagining how we show love, we lay the foundation for generations to come—a legacy rooted in warmth, understanding, and unwavering support. In doing so, we transform our lives and pave the way for future generations to experience love that unshackles rather than confines—a love that truly knows no bounds.

REFLECTION JOURNAL PROMPTS

Take a deep breath....
These are just for you. There is no pressure to have the perfect
answer—write what comes to mind.

Includes Powerful Reflection Journal Prompts
The Moment I Knew I Didn't Want to Parent Like I
Was Raised":

1. What specific experience or moment made you realize
   that the way you were raised didn't align with the kind
   of parent you wanted to become?

2. How did your emotional response in that moment
   influence the changes you made in your parenting
   style?

3. What core values or beliefs emerged for you at that
   moment that now guide how you raise your children
   differently?

4. What would I say if I could speak to my younger self in
   a moment of pain?

5. What part of me feels triggered when my child pushes
   my buttons?

"Yelling Was My Default Language—Until I Heard
Myself":

1. What did you notice or feel the first time you heard
   yourself yelling, and how did it shift your perspective on
   your behavior?

2. What do you think yelling was trying to express for you that words couldn't, and how have you begun to replace it with more effective communication?

3. What impact did your yelling have on your relationships, and what changes have you seen since becoming more aware of your tone and reactions?

4. Which protective parts of me still take the lead when I'm under stress?

5. How does your body feel?

"Unlearning Love That Hurt: Affection Without Fear":

1. When did you first realize that some of the ways love was shown to you growing up were rooted in fear, control, or pain rather than genuine care?

2. What steps have you taken to redefine love in your life to feel safe, nurturing, and unconditional for yourself and others?

3. How has your journey of unlearning painful expressions of love shaped how you now offer affection, especially to your children or close relationships?

4. What would that version of me want to hear most?

5. What beliefs about parenting did I inherit that I'm beginning to question?

CHAPTER 2

UNDERSTANDING EMOTIONAL LANDSCAPES

Building Your Emotional Toolbox

Picture this: you're in the middle of a parenting whirlwind, juggling the chaos of breakfast, lunch prep, and a toddler's tantrum. Suddenly, you feel that familiar surge of frustration. In these moments, wouldn't it be great to reach into an emotional toolbox, whip out a trusty tool, and restore calm? An emotional toolbox is a set of skills and strategies to handle these emotional challenges effectively. It's like having a Swiss Army knife for your feelings, ready to help you navigate the emotional rollercoaster of parenting with poise and grace.

Self-awareness, self-regulation, and empathy are the cornerstones of your emotional toolbox. Self-awareness is understanding what makes you tick—recognizing patterns and triggers in your emotional responses. Self-regulation is managing those emotions, even when your toddler has a third-morning meltdown. Empathy involves stepping into someone else's shoes and trying to understand the world from their perspective. Together, these skills form a powerful trio that can transform your interactions with your children and yourself.

To sharpen self-awareness, consider integrating meditation practices into your routine. Set aside a few minutes daily to sit quietly, focusing on your breath and observing your thoughts as they drift by like clouds. This practice enhances your ability to recognize emotional patterns and respond rather than react impulsively. Another effective tool is keeping an emotion journal. You gain insights into your emotional landscape by tracking your daily mood changes and noting what triggers specific emotions. It's like keeping a weather diary for your mind—one day might be sunny, the next cloudy with a chance of showers.

When it comes to emotional regulation, breathing exercises can be a lifesaver. Picture this: you're standing in a checkout line, and your kid is on the verge of a meltdown because you said no to candy. Before panic sets in, pause and take a deep breath.

Breathe for four counts, hold for four, then exhale for four. This simple exercise can help restore calm and clarity in moments of stress. Visualization techniques also work wonders. Picture yourself in a serene environment—maybe a beach or a quiet forest—and let that mental image guide you back to a place of peace.

As you build your emotional toolbox, remember it's a work in progress. Continual learning and adaptation are key. To expand your range of tools, consider attending workshops on emotional intelligence or reading books on personal development. The more you learn, the more equipped you'll be to handle whatever life throws your way.

Reflection Exercise

Take fifteen minutes each week to engage in a reflection exercise. Find a quiet space and jot down any new insights or tools you've discovered that week. Reflect on what worked well and what could use some tweaking. This practice not only reinforces learning but also helps you adapt as needed.

Building and improving an emotional toolbox is similar to investing in yourself—it's about equipping yourself with the resources needed to thrive as a parent and human being. The tools may vary depending on the situation, but their primary goal is to foster resilience in adversity.

Emotional intelligence isn't just about managing emotions; it's also about creating connections with those around us. We strengthen our bonds with them by approaching our children with empathy and understanding instead of judgment or frustration. We create an environment where they feel safe expressing themselves without fear of judgment.

Incorporating these skills into daily life requires practice but yields immense rewards—improved relationships with your children, enhanced personal well-being, and increased capacity for joy amid life's challenges. It's about showing up fully present for yourself and those you love, embracing the highs and lows with open arms.

Remember that this journey toward greater self-awareness and emotional regulation doesn't demand perfection; instead, it asks for progress—a willingness to learn from missteps while celebrating small victories. So, here's to building an emotional toolbox that empowers us as parents and individuals to navigate life's complexities with grace.

As you navigate this chapter on understanding emotional landscapes, may these insights serve as guiding lights illuminating paths toward a more profound connection with yourself and others—a reminder that even amid chaos lies the opportunity for growth and transformation.

Recognizing Triggers: The Path to Emotional Awareness

We all have those moments when something small sets us off, like a match to a fuse. Suddenly, we're in a full-blown emotional reaction before we know what's hit us. These are our emotional triggers—those pesky little buttons that, when pressed, can send our emotions spiraling. Criticism is common; even the slightest hint can feel like a personal attack, leaving us defensive or angry. Disrespect is another heavyweight champ in the trigger arena, often evoking feelings of worthlessness or anger. Understanding these triggers is crucial because they don't just influence our behavior—they control it. Unchecked, they dictate our responses and interactions, often leading to conflicts or misunderstandings.

Identifying personal triggers requires some detective work. It's about playing Sherlock Holmes with your emotional history. Reflecting on past conflicts can reveal recurring themes—those moments where you reacted strongly and later wondered why. Was it something someone said or did? Is there a pattern? Mindfulness helps here, too. You can catch those triggers by paying attention to your physical and emotional reactions. Notice when your chest tightens, or your fists clench. These are clues pointing to deeper emotional currents at play. They help you identify what sets you off so you can start taking back control.

Managing reactions to triggers involves creating space between the stimulus and your response—a pause that allows you to choose how to react instead of acting on impulse. Picture this: you're in a heated conversation, and someone says something triggering. Before responding, take a moment to breathe deeply. This pause allows your brain to catch up with your emotions, letting you respond more thoughtfully. Developing a personal mantra can also work wonders—a simple phrase that grounds you and helps you regain composure *(I like to use I'm a good dad)*. It could be as straightforward as "I am calm" or "This too shall pass." Repeating it silently can diffuse the emotional charge, giving you the clarity to respond effectively.

Seeing triggers as opportunities for growth is where the magic happens. It's about transforming them from pesky annoyances into valuable teachers. Journaling is a powerful tool here. By writing about your triggers, you explore the underlying beliefs that give them power. Maybe criticism stings because, deep down, you fear not being good enough. By unraveling these beliefs, you gain insight into your emotional landscape and can work on changing those narratives. Seeking feedback from trusted friends or family provides another perspective on your triggers. They can offer insights you might overlook, helping you produce self-awareness and understanding.

Developing Emotional Intelligence: The Key to Connection

Emotional intelligence is the secret sauce that flavors our interactions with empathy and understanding. At its core, it's about recognizing and managing our own emotions while tuning into the feelings of others. It involves self-awareness— knowing what we feel and why—alongside self-regulation, which keeps those emotions in check. It also includes motivation, empathy, and social skills, which are crucial for building meaningful relationships.

Emotional intelligence is like a superpower in parenting. It helps us connect with our kids more deeply by using empathy to see the world through their eyes. Understanding their feelings and experiences enhances communication through emotional harmony—responding with sensitivity and support rather than judgment or frustration.

Calming emotional intelligence takes practice. Role-playing scenarios with your kids can boost empathy by letting you step into their shoes and see things from their perspective. Active listening exercises with family members strengthen emotional bonds by showing that you value their thoughts and feelings. It's about being fully present and engaged in conversations without interrupting or judging.

Measuring emotional growth is all about examining your progress over time. Reflective journaling about your emotional interactions can illuminate how your understanding has developed. Plus, seeking regular feedback from family and friends can give you a helpful outside perspective on how well you connect emotionally with those around you.

The Empathy Muscle: Strengthening Family Bonds

Empathy is like a muscle—it needs regular exercise to stay strong. It's not just about feeling sorry for someone; it's about truly understanding their experience from their point of view. Practicing empathy in daily life involves engaging in acts of kindness and listening deeply during family discussions without interrupting or offering unwanted advice.

In parenting, empathy enhances our ability to respond compassionately during conflicts by first understanding our children's emotional needs. When children feel heard and understood, they're more likely to share their feelings and experiences.

Overcoming empathy barriers requires recognizing personal biases that may cloud our judgment and practicing self-care to maintain empathetic capacity. It's about acknowledging our limitations while striving to expand our ability to connect with others on an emotional level.

Emotional Bandwidth: Expanding Your Capacity for Love

Emotional bandwidth refers to our capacity to handle emotional demands without feeling overwhelmed. It's linked closely with resilience—the ability to bounce back from adversity stronger than before. Expanding this bandwidth requires prioritizing self-care practices that prevent burnout while delegating tasks whenever possible.

Balancing emotional demands involves setting realistic expectations for yourself and your family while establishing boundaries that protect your emotional health. This balance allows for more patience and understanding when interacting with loved ones.

The benefits of expanded bandwidth are immense. More extraordinary patience in parenting leads to more harmonious family dynamics while enhancing one's ability to enjoy interactions entirely without feeling drained or depleted. Imagine fitting a gallon of emotions into a pint-sized jar—frustrating, right? That's where the concept of emotional bandwidth comes into play. Think of it like your phone's data plan. Once you hit your limit, everything slows down, and you may drop a call or two. Emotional bandwidth is similar; it's your capacity to handle emotional demands without exceeding your limit. When we increase this capacity, we build resilience—a sort of emotional elasticity that helps us bounce back from adversity and stress without snapping. Emotional bandwidth isn't static; it can be expanded with intention and practice, allowing us to better absorb life's ups and downs.

Expanding your emotional bandwidth starts with self-care. It's like refueling your car; you're going nowhere fast without it. Make sure to carve out time for activities that recharge your batteries. Whether reading, exercising, or enjoying coffee in peace, these moments prevent burnout and replenish your emotional reserves. Delegating tasks is another trick to lighten the load. You don't have to be a superhero trying to do it all. Share responsibilities at home and work when possible. It's okay to ask for help—you're not losing control but gaining support. These strategies create space for emotional growth, helping you handle more without feeling overwhelmed.

We often set the bar high, expecting perfection in our parenting and personal lives. But let's face it—perfection is a myth. Accepting that some days will be messy *(literally and figuratively)* helps alleviate pressure and stress. Establishing boundaries is crucial, too. It's okay to say no when needed or take a step back from commitments that drain rather than fulfill you. These boundaries safeguard your emotional bandwidth, allowing you to focus on what truly matters.

With greater capacity comes more incredible patience and understanding in parenting. You'll be less reactive during those unavoidable toddler tantrums or teenage eye rolls. Instead of snapping, you'll approach situations calmly and clearly, leading to more peaceful interactions at home. Enhanced emotional capacity also means you can enjoy family time more fully. You'll be present physically and emotionally, engaging with your loved ones rather than being distracted by stress or anxiety.

As we expand our emotional bandwidth, we open ourselves to deeper connections with those around us. We become more attuned to our family's needs, responding with empathy and compassion even in challenging times. This heightened awareness fosters stronger bonds built on trust and mutual support.

In closing this chapter on understanding emotional landscapes, remember that expanding your emotional bandwidth is not about achieving more but being more present in each moment. It's about creating space within yourself for love—to receive it from others and give it freely in return.

As we move into the next chapter, consider what steps you can take today to expand your art of hearing beyond words. Being fully present in such moments demands more than a casual glance or shared space. With increased emotional bandwidth, we navigate life's challenges with resilience, embracing its joys and trials with open hearts, ready for whatever comes our way. So here's to expanding our capacity for love, one intentional step at a time.

REFLECTION JOURNAL PROMPTS

Take a deep breath....

These are just for you. There is no pressure to have the perfect answer—write what comes to mind.

"Understanding Emotional Landscapes":

1. What emotions dominate your inner world, and how do they shape how you respond to stress, connection, or conflict?

2. How were emotions talked about—or not talked about—in your upbringing, and how has that influenced your current emotional awareness?

3. What patterns have you noticed in your emotional responses, and what tools or insights have helped you navigate them more mindfully?

"Recognizing Triggers: The Path to Emotional Awareness":

1. Can you recall a recent moment when you felt intensely triggered—what was happening, and what more profound emotion or memory might have been activated?

2. How do your body and mind typically react when triggered, and what helps you slow down and respond rather than react?

3. What patterns have you discovered in your triggers, and how are they connected to past experiences or unmet needs?

"Emotional Bandwidth: Expanding Your Capacity for Love":

1. What does it feel like when your emotional bandwidth is stretched thin, and how do you recognize when you're nearing that limit?
2. What practices or boundaries have helped you expand your ability to hold space for love for yourself and others?
3. How has increasing your emotional capacity changed how you connect in your relationships, especially during stress or vulnerability?

"Developing Emotional Intelligence: The Key to Connection":

1. How has becoming more aware of your emotions changed how you relate to others daily?
2. What challenges have you faced in identifying or expressing your feelings, and how have you worked to overcome them?
3. In what ways has developing empathy and emotional understanding deepened your connections with your children, partner, or community?

CHAPTER 3

COMMUNICATION BRIDGES

Active Listening: The Art of Hearing Beyond Words

We've all been there, haven't we? You're engaged in the day-to-day whirlwind, spinning plates and juggling tasks like a seasoned circus performer, when your child approaches with something to share. You find yourself nodding along, tossing in an occasional "really?" or "wow," all the while your mind is miles away, caught up in the plethora of other pressing concerns. This scenario highlights where active listening steps in—a transformative tool for any parent hoping to enhance their relationship with their child. Active listening transcends the simple act of hearing words; it encapsulates the essence of being present, so present that you tune into the emotional frequency your child emits.

Active listening requires a profound focus on the spoken words and the unsaid—the subtle non-verbal communication conveyed through actions, body language, and facial expressions, which often speak volumes. Being fully present in such moments demands more than a casual glance or shared space. It means consciously setting aside external distractions: putting down the phone, turning off the TV, and granting your child your complete, undivided attention. Consider the power of making meaningful eye contact, nodding to demonstrate your engagement, and using your body language to reflect your interest.

Observing their eyes light up as they describe their day or noting how their shoulders slump when they mention a problem are vital indicators, serving as breadcrumbs that pave the path to a deeper, more profound understanding.

Improving your active listening skills can elevate your connection. Begin by paraphrasing your child's words to ensure clarity and mutual understanding. For instance, they may share a story about their school day filled with challenges, reiterating it to them, "So you're saying that the science project was more challenging than you thought?" reaffirms your attentiveness and encourages them to delve deeper into the topic. Reflective listening further enhances this skill. By restating what you believe they are feeling, you engage in an empathetic confirmation process: "It sounds like you were frustrated today."

This acknowledges their feelings and offers them a framework to understand and name their emotions, which they may not fully grasp.

However, barriers to active listening can sprout unexpectedly, much like weeds in an otherwise pristine garden. Distractions emerge as the most common obstacles; the incessant buzzing of phones, the persistent ding of emails, and the ever-present to-do list often struggle for attention. Creating a distraction-free zone during conversations is crucial yet challenging. It may seem daunting, but dedicating even a mere ten minutes to an undisturbed, focused talk can perform wonders for your relationship. Preconceived notions also pose a risk. We might often assume that we know what our children will say because, let's face it, kids can be predictable. Approaching each conversation with a clean slate, without assumptions, unlocks doors to genuine, authentic understanding.

Regularly engaging in active listening is fundamental to building and reinforcing robust family communication bridges. Establish designated times for one-on-one conversations—perhaps during bedtime routines or after dinner. Make this formal; let your child know they're valued and their thoughts and feelings are essential. This dedicated time reinforces that they have your full, undivided attention and fosters an environment where they feel heard.

Reflection Exercise

Give this a try:

Choose a specific time each week to engage in a distraction-free conversation with your child, perhaps during breakfast or while enjoying a walk in the park. Immerse yourself completely in the listening process—paraphrase their words to show comprehension, acknowledge their emotions empathetically, and maintain eye contact to solidify the connection. Afterwards, take a moment to reflect on how this practice influenced your interaction and observe any shifts in your relationship dynamics with your child.

Through active listening, we transform ordinary exchanges into profound, meaningful dialogues that nurture trust and connection within the family unit. This practice extends beyond just constructing bridges; it's about upholding and reinforcing them, ensuring they remain steadfast and resilient enough to weather the inevitable storms life might present.

Empathetic Responses: Speaking the Language of Love

Ever tried speaking to someone who just doesn't get it? It's like talking to a wall. Now, imagine your child feels that way—often. That's where empathy swoops in as a superhero in family dynamics. Empathetic communication isn't just about giving a nod and a smile; it's about recognizing and validating children's feelings. It's the heartfelt "I understand" that bridges gaps and mends fences. When your child comes to you with a problem, they're not seeking solutions as much as reassurance. They're looking for someone to acknowledge their emotions, to tell them, "I see you, and it's okay to feel this way."

Crafting empathetic responses is an art form. It involves using "I" statements that express understanding without judgment. Instead of saying, "You're overreacting," try, "I see that you're upset, and I can imagine how tough that must feel." These statements shift the focus from judgment to understanding, creating a safe space for dialogue. Dismissive language can shut down communication quicker than a slammed door. Instead, using compassionate language invites open conversations. When your child tells you about their day, good or bad, respond with curiosity and warmth. "Tell me more about what happened," encourages them to open up rather than retreat into silence.

Empathy plays a crucial role in resolving conflicts and fortifying relationships. Imagine two kids in a heated argument over a toy. One empathetic response can de-escalate the situation faster than you can say "timeout." By acknowledging both sides and validating emotions, you create common ground. "I see you're both passionate about this toy. Let's figure out how everyone can enjoy it." This approach calms the storm and teaches your children the value of empathy in resolving disagreements.

Some exercises can make enhancing empathy within the family second nature. Role-playing scenarios where each family member takes on different roles can help practice empathetic dialogue. It's like a mini-theater production where everyone gets to walk in someone else's shoes for a while. Sharing personal stories also fosters connection. Sharing experiences from your life opens the door for your children to understand that you were once in their shoes, too.

Empathy isn't just a skill; it's a lifestyle choice that brings families closer together. It requires patience, practice, and persistence, but pays off with stronger bonds and healthier interactions. Imagine your home as a garden where empathy is the water that nourishes every relationship, helping it grow and flourish with love and understanding.

Incorporating empathy into everyday interactions means more than just responding thoughtfully; it means living it. It's about being present when your child needs you, even if it means pausing your favourite TV show or stepping away from an important work email. Those moments of connection are the building blocks of a strong family foundation. They teach your children that love isn't just words; it's actions, and sometimes, it's the quiet presence that speaks louder than any words could.

As we continue this communication journey, remember that empathy is an ongoing practice—a dance between hearts where each step brings us closer together. Embrace it with open arms and watch your family transform into a unit bound by love and understanding.

Vulnerability as Strength: Sharing Your Inner World

You know, there's something incredibly freeing about letting down your guard. Vulnerability has often been painted as a weakness, something to avoid. But imagine this: a father sitting with his child, sharing stories of triumphs and struggles, too.

There's power in that openness. Being vulnerable means showing your true self with all the cracks and imperfections, and that's where genuine connection begins. It's like opening the windows in a stuffy room, letting fresh air sweep through. In recent years, our culture has gradually shifted toward embracing emotional openness, slowly but surely dismantling the walls that once stood so high and mighty. We've seen public figures and celebrities championing this cause, creating a ripple effect that encourages everyone to shed that outdated armour.

The benefits of being vulnerable with your children are profound and numerous. It builds an atmosphere of trust where communication flows freely, like a two-way street unimpeded by traffic jams. When you share your feelings and experiences, you model emotional authenticity, showing them it's okay to feel and express themselves openly. It's like giving them a map for navigating their emotional landscapes. They start seeing you not just as the one who enforces bedtime rules or serves up broccoli without fail but as a fellow human with fears, dreams, and emotions. This authenticity fosters a relationship where they feel safe to share their inner worlds without fear of judgment or misunderstanding.

So, how does one embrace vulnerability comfortably? It starts small, like dipping your toes into a pool before the full plunge. Gradually share personal experiences with your children, perhaps when you faced a challenge or felt uncertain about something. You might say, "I was nervous before my big presentation at work." This sharing also invites them to open up, creating a space where reciprocal vulnerability thrives. Please encourage them to share their thoughts and feelings, ensuring no subject is off-limits. Over time, these exchanges become the foundation of a deep, enduring connection grounded in mutual understanding.

Of course, navigating the terrain of vulnerability isn't without its challenges. It can feel like walking a tightrope—balancing openness with the need for boundaries. You don't have to overshare or lay every thought bare; instead, choose what feels correct and appropriate for the moment. Setting boundaries is crucial for maintaining comfort while still being open. Remember, keeping some things private or sharing certain feelings only when ready is okay. Seeking support from partners or peers can also be invaluable when embracing vulnerability feels daunting. Having someone to talk to about your experiences and emotions adds an extra layer of support, reminding you that you're not alone in this endeavour.

Embracing vulnerability is an ongoing process, like tending to a delicate garden. It requires patience and care but yields immense rewards through stronger relationships and deeper connections with your children. As you share your inner world with them, you'll notice changes in how they relate to you and carry themselves. They learn that being open isn't something to fear but cherish—a strength rather than a weakness.

So here's to redefining vulnerability as the powerful force it truly is. Let's challenge those outdated notions and embrace emotional openness as an integral part of our relationships. Let's show our children that being human means connecting deeply and authentically. As we continue this path together, remember that each step towards vulnerability is one towards building bridges—bridges made not of stone but of shared stories and heartfelt understanding.

Overcoming the Fear of Emotional Expression

Picture a father deeply entrenched in family life and career responsibilities, who hesitates to express his emotions, keeping them tucked away like old photos in a forgotten album, relegated to the dim sidelines of his consciousness. This reluctance, which echoes through countless generations, often stems from deep-rooted societal expectations—those age-old beliefs and cultural constructs that dictate how men should behave. Men are traditionally seen as pillars of strength, models of impassiveness, and paragons of endurance, ideally impervious to any form of emotional turbulence that might sway their resolve. Growing up, many of us were subtly taught and gently nudged to embrace the saying that showing emotions was similar to revealing weakness, a lesson continued by the prevailing media, influenced by daring cultural narratives where vulnerability is neither an option nor a consideration.

Past experiences serve as vivid reminders of emotional suppression, where vulnerability was met with ridicule, judgment, or casual dismissal. Memories of feeling exposed or having emotions belittled linger in the mind, adding another layer to the fear of emotional expression—a tightly wound barrier that can stifle open and honest communication.

However, fear is not an unmovable obstacle. It's not cemented in stability, and its roots can be carefully loosened. Confronting it—this daunting spectre of emotional expression—begins with challenging those negative, deeply ingrained beliefs about emotions. Recognize and acknowledge, perhaps for the first time consciously, that emotions aren't markers of fragility, no more so than a roof over your head signifies insecurity. Instead, they are vivid signals of humanity, instinctual connections to our deeper selves and those around us, allowing for authentic interactions that are both fulfilling and enriching.

Gradually exposing oneself to emotional expression can also help transform fear into acceptance. Begin by sharing small snippets of feelings in safe and trusted environments—perhaps during a quiet moment, discussing a moving book or film with your child, and gently expressing how it made you feel. Over time, these small, seemingly insignificant steps gradually build confidence, making emotional openness feel natural and less daunting, like learning to swim with flotation aids until ready to take the plunge unaided.

Open emotional expression plays a vitally important role in father-child relationships. It acts as a bridge—a symbolic roadway—to deeper understanding and empathy. When you express your emotions openly and without reservation, you invite your child into that space, encouraging them to do the same. This act fosters an environment where feelings are acknowledged, respected, and cherished. It's akin to opening a window in a stuffy room, allowing the fresh, invigorating air to circulate and breathe new life into interactions. This mutual acceptance and understanding encourage children to express their emotions freely, liberated from the fear of judgment, creating a family dynamic that thrives on trust, transparency, and empathy.

Supportive practices can further nurture an atmosphere where emotional expression can thrive and blossom. Consider creating enriching family rituals that celebrate emotions, perhaps through a weekly "feelings check-in" where everyone around the table, regardless of age or disposition, shares their highs and lows from the week. These rituals help normalize emotional discussion, making it a regular, welcomed part of family life. Art and music can also serve as powerful, transformative outlets for emotional expression. Please encourage your children to draw or paint their feelings on canvases or create playlists reflecting their moods. These creative endeavours offer alternative, profound ways to express emotions, sometimes articulating what words cannot.

Imagine a world, a society, where expressing emotions is as routine as brushing your teeth or smiling at a neighbour in the morning. It may sound far-fetched, utopian, even, but with consistent practice and steadfast dedication, it becomes a second-nature ability we carry into every interaction. The benefits ripple outwards, influencing personal relationships, enhancing overall well-being, and building resilience. Emotional expression enriches our lives, allowing us to experience the full, vibrant spectrum of human emotion without fear or restraint. It's about embracing the nuanced messiness of life with open arms, accepting that feeling deeply and expressing those feelings is part of what makes us authentically human.

So here's to overcoming the fear of emotional expression—tearing down those outdated, stubborn notions and welcoming vulnerability as a cherished friend rather than an adversary to dread. By doing so, we create warm, inviting spaces where love, understanding, and genuine connection flourish, where emotions are celebrated rather than shunned. Let's embark on this collective adventure toward more open, honest, and heartfelt communication within our families, drawing strength and solidarity from the shared human experience.

Creating a Dialogue of Trust with Your Children

Building trust is like planting a garden. It requires patience, consistency, and a lot of nurturing. In the realm of father-child communication, trust is the soil where everything else grows. Without it, conversations become surface-level exchanges, lacking depth and authenticity. Consistency and reliability are the cornerstones of this trust. When you consistently show up, keep your promises, and follow through on commitments, you create a stable environment where your child feels safe to open up. Honesty plays a pivotal role here. Being transparent about your feelings and intentions sets the stage for them to do the same. It's not just about being truthful; it's about creating a space where truth feels welcome.

Establishing trust takes more than words; it's an active process involving listening and respecting boundaries. Active listening can make your child feel heard and valued. When they see you genuinely engaging with their thoughts and feelings, it builds a foundation of trust that encourages them to share more. Setting boundaries is equally important. Respecting their independence and privacy while ensuring they feel secure is crucial. This balance fosters an environment where they can express themselves without fear of judgment or invasion. Trust isn't built overnight; it's a continuous process of demonstrating respect, understanding, and unwavering support.

But what happens when trust falters? Addressing and repairing breaches is crucial to restoring harmony in the relationship. Mistakes are inevitable, but how you handle them can make all the difference. Apologies should be sincere, acknowledging any hurt caused and expressing a genuine desire to make amends. Words alone aren't enough; actions speak louder. Rebuilding trust requires consistent behaviour that aligns with your promises. Show them through your actions that you're committed to making things right. This process reinforces the idea that while mistakes happen, they don't define the relationship.

Encouraging open communication is about creating a dialogue where your child feels comfortable sharing their thoughts and emotions. Regular family meetings can be a platform for discussing issues and celebrating successes. These gatherings reinforce the idea that every voice matters, promoting a sense of belonging and importance within the family unit. Encourage questions and discussions about complex topics—school challenges or world events—to foster intellectual curiosity and emotional openness. Their eagerness to engage in meaningful conversations signals their opinions are valued and respected.

Communication isn't just an exchange of words; it's a bridge that connects hearts and minds. As fathers, we can model authentic communication, prioritizing trust, empathy, and openness. It's about being present in those everyday moments when your child needs you most, whether it's listening to their latest school escapade or discussing their fears about the future. These interactions lay the groundwork for a relationship built on mutual respect and love.

As you continue nurturing this dialogue of trust with your children, remember that small steps lead to significant change over time. Each conversation becomes a building block in your relationship—a testament to the power of authentic communication in strengthening family bonds.

As we wrap up this chapter on communication bridges, let's apply these insights to our daily interactions with our children. Remember that trust is both the starting point and destination of meaningful communication—a cycle that enriches our lives and those of our loved ones.

The next chapter will explore practical strategies for breaking cycles of dysfunction. We will embrace challenges as opportunities for growth and learning together as we navigate life's ups and downs.

REFLECTION JOURNAL PROMPTS

Take a deep breath....

These are just for you. There is no pressure to have the perfect answer—write what comes to mind.

"Active Listening: The Art of Hearing Beyond Words":

1. When was the last time you felt truly heard by someone, and what made that experience stand out to you?
2. How do you stay present and open during conversations, especially when emotions are high or the topic is challenging?
3. What have you learned about others and yourself by practicing active listening instead of jumping to respond or fix?

"Empathetic Responses: Speaking the Language of Love":

1. How do you know when someone needs empathy rather than advice, and how do you respond accordingly?
2. What does it look like to respond with love, especially when you feel triggered, frustrated, or misunderstood?
3. How has learning to speak with empathy changed the dynamics in your close relationships, especially with your children or partner?

"Vulnerability as Strength: Sharing Your Inner World":

1.   What fears come up when you consider being emotionally vulnerable, and where do you think those fears originated?
2.   Can you recall when opening up created a more profound connection—what did you share, and how was it received?
3.   How has embracing vulnerability reshaped your understanding of strength in relationships and parenting?

"Overcoming the Fear of Emotional Expression":

1.   What messages did you receive growing up about expressing emotions, and how have those messages shaped your current fears around emotional openness?
2.   What emotions do you find hardest to express, and what do you think lies beneath that difficulty?
3.   What small steps have helped—or could help—you feel safer expressing your true feelings with others?

"Creating a Dialogue of Trust with Your Children":

1. What moments have shown you that your child feels safe opening up to you, and what helped build that trust?

2. How do you respond when your child shares something complex or unexpected, and how might that response impact their willingness to keep sharing?

3. What daily practices or habits could you use to foster a more open, judgment-free space for communication with your child?

CHAPTER 4

BREAKING CYCLES OF DYSFUNCTION

Identifying Patterns: The First Step to Change

Picture your family dinner scene, where the familiar bickering over who gets the last slice of pizza unfolds. Surprised at how often this plays out, you raise your voice. Identifying these recurring patterns is like dusting off an old film reel and hitting play. It's about recognizing the scenes that replay, often unnoticed yet deeply ingrained in the family dynamic. Recognizing dysfunctional patterns is the first step toward change. You might notice that specific interactions trigger emotional responses—perhaps a tone of voice or a particular word. Maybe it's how conflict arises over minor issues, like dishes left in the sink or mismatched socks.

Reflect on family interactions that set off these emotional alarms. Consider the times you've felt your heart rate spike or your patience thin out like a stretched rubber band. Analyze past family conflicts for recurring themes. Is there a pattern of avoidance where issues are swept under the rug like dust bunnies? Or is there a tendency for voices to rise until everyone shouts over each other? Unraveling these threads helps you understand what happens and why it happens, laying the groundwork for transformation.

Tools for self-reflection come in handy here, like magnifying glasses for your soul. Keeping a reflection journal is one method that allows you to track behavioral patterns over time. Jot down moments when you feel a strong emotional response, noting what triggered it and how you reacted. Over time, these entries reveal patterns you might not have noticed in the daily hustle. Engaging in guided self-assessment exercises can further uncover ingrained behaviors and attitudes. These exercises ask questions like, "What's my gut reaction in tense situations?" and "How does my past influence my present decisions?"

Understanding the origins of these patterns is crucial for meaningful change. It's like peeling back the layers of an onion, revealing the core beliefs and values inherited from your family history. Exploring family history offers insight into current behaviors—maybe your tendency to avoid conflict stems from witnessing unresolved tension in your childhood home. Identifying inherited beliefs that no longer serve paves the way for new narratives. Perhaps there's an unspoken rule about not showing vulnerability because it's seen as a weakness.

Setting the stage for transformation involves creating a personal commitment to change—a mental contract with yourself that says, "I'm ready to break free from these cycles." Share your intentions with family members to foster accountability and support. Let them know you're working on being more present during conversations or handling conflicts differently. This transparency invites them into your journey, encouraging collaboration rather than resistance.

Reflection Exercise

Set aside time each week to write in your reflection journal. Focus on interactions that stir strong emotions and analyze them for patterns or triggers. Ask yourself what beliefs influenced your reactions, and consider how you'd like to respond differently next time.

Breaking cycles of dysfunction isn't just about identifying problems; it's about envisioning possibilities. It's about taking those old film reels and rewriting the script, scene by scene. As you embark on this path, remember that change doesn't demand perfection but progress—a willingness to look within and make conscious choices moving forward.

The journey won't always be easy; there will be moments when old habits try to sneak back in, whispering familiar lines from scripts you're determined to rewrite. But with each step toward understanding and transformation, you forge a new path defined by intention, empathy, and growth.

By embracing this process, you create space for healthier dynamics rooted in authenticity rather than fear or dysfunction. In doing so, you lay the foundation for future generations—a legacy built on love, understanding, and resilience.

Stepping into this role is an honor and a challenge, but it's worth taking on with courage and compassion. Together, we can break free from the chains of dysfunction and build families where love thrives without reservation or limitation.

So, let's dive deep into our stories with open hearts ready for change—a journey toward healing that begins by simply recognizing where we've been so we can choose where we're going next.

Conscious Parenting: Making Intentional Choices

Imagine waking up each day with a clear sense of purpose in your parenting, where every choice you make is deliberate and aligned with the home you wish to create. Conscious parenting is about doing just that. It's about being aware and intentional, like a gardener tending to a delicate plant, knowing that your actions today shape tomorrow's growth. At its core, conscious parenting prioritizes the emotional well-being of your children. It asks you to pause, reflect, and consider how your actions affect the little humans in your care. It's not about being perfect but about being present and understanding that each interaction is an opportunity to build trust and nurture love.

In practice, intentional parenting involves setting clear family values and goals. These guiding stars keep you on course, even during stormy seas. You may value honesty, kindness, and resilience. Articulate these values as a family, over dinner, or on a weekend walk. This shared vision helps align your actions with your principles, ensuring everyone is on the same page. Incorporate mindfulness into daily routines to remain grounded. This could be as simple as taking a few deep breaths before responding to a tantrum or practicing gratitude during breakfast. These small acts of mindfulness help maintain focus on what truly matters.

Balancing discipline with compassion is another pillar of conscious parenting. It's about understanding that discipline isn't synonymous with punishment. Instead of disciplinary measures, consider positive reinforcement—praising efforts rather than solely focusing on results. When a child does something praiseworthy, acknowledge it with specific feedback: "I noticed how hard you worked on your homework—that's impressive!" This approach encourages growth and builds self-esteem. Open dialogue about consequences is equally crucial. When rules are broken, discuss the impact of actions rather than resorting to immediate punishment. Ask questions like, "How do you think your actions affected others?" This encourages reflection and accountability while fostering empathy.

Creating a supportive family environment requires intentional effort. Establish routines that promote stability, like regular mealtimes or bedtime rituals, providing a sense of security amidst life's unpredictability. Encourage family activities that build connections and strengthen bonds. Whether it's a weekly game night or a monthly outing to explore nature, these shared experiences become cherished memories and opportunities for genuine connection. They remind everyone involved that family isn't just about living together but growing together.

Conscious parenting is not an overnight transformation but a series of small, thoughtful choices made consistently over time. It's about being present in each moment, choosing love over fear, and understanding that your actions today lay the foundation for tomorrow's family dynamics. As you navigate this path, remember that mistakes are part of the process—they provide valuable lessons for growth and adaptation.

One effective way to incorporate conscious parenting into daily life is to create an intention-setting ritual each morning. Take a moment to visualize how you'd like the day to unfold with your children—what qualities would you like to embody? Patience? Empathy? Write down these intentions or repeat them aloud as affirmations throughout the day. This practice gently reminds you of your commitment to intentionality amid daily chaos.

Another strategy involves connecting children in decision-making processes where appropriate. This empowers them by giving them a voice in matters affecting their lives while teaching responsibility and collaboration skills. For instance, when planning meals or family outings, invite input from everyone involved, allowing them to feel valued and heard within the family unit.

Remember that conscious parenting extends beyond interactions with children; it encompasses self-care practices essential for maintaining emotional well-being. I prioritize time for activities that recharge my energy levels—exercise, reading, or simply enjoying solitude with a cup of tea or coffee!

By embracing conscious parenting practices, you'll find yourself navigating challenges with greater ease while nurturing deeper connections with those who matter most—your children—and creating an environment where love thrives unconditionally without reservation or judgment.

So here's to making intentional daily choices—to choosing presence over perfection—and building families rooted in empathy, understanding, and unwavering support as we journey through life's beautiful complexities together.

Cycle Breaker: Embracing the Role of Change Agent

Stepping into the role of a cycle breaker is like taking on the mantle of a family superhero, although without a cape, but with plenty of courage. It's about accepting the responsibility to alter family dynamics that have long been dysfunctional. Picture this: you are standing at the helm of your family ship, steering it away from the rocky shoals of past behaviors and toward the calm waters of understanding and care. Acknowledge that while this role requires effort, it also offers the chance to redefine what family means for you and your loved ones.

Being a change agent involves viewing yourself as a leader in family transformation. It's about setting the tone for healthier interactions and relationships. Start by implementing small, consistent changes in daily interactions. It could be as simple as greeting each family member with a smile each morning or taking a few moments to listen when someone shares their day.

These small actions build up over time, creating a ripple effect that encourages others to follow suit.

Encouraging family discussions on desired changes is another step in fostering meaningful transformation. These discussions can be informal chats over dinner or more structured family meetings. The key is to create a space where everyone feels safe expressing their thoughts and hopes for what family life could be like. By doing so, you not only foster open communication but also empower each member to take part in shaping the family's future.

Resistance from family members is natural; it's like trying to introduce broccoli at a dessert buffet. Communicate the benefits of change to your family in relatable terms. Explain how these changes aim to make life better for everyone, reducing stress and promoting happiness. Patience and persistence are crucial here. When faced with resistance, remember that change takes time and that setbacks are part of the process. Keep showing up with kindness and understanding, even when things get tough.

Celebrating milestones is an integral part of this transformation journey. It's about recognizing the progress made and honoring the successes achieved along the way. Create family rituals to celebrate these achievements, whether a special dinner, a homemade certificate ceremony, or simply sharing words of appreciation during a weekly family meeting. These celebrations reinforce positive changes and motivate everyone to keep moving forward.

Reflecting on personal growth is equally crucial since embracing this role. Consider how far you've come and what you've learned about yourself and your family dynamics. This reflection can be done through journaling or simply meditating on your journey over a cup of coffee. Acknowledge the challenges overcome and the strengths developed along the way. This practice boosts your confidence and reinforces your commitment to continued growth and positive change.

In embracing the role of cycle breaker, you become a beacon of hope and possibility within your family. You demonstrate that change is possible and achievable with intention and perseverance. Your actions inspire others to join you in creating a healthier, more harmonious family environment where love and understanding thrive.

The journey ahead may be filled with twists and turns, yet each step forward brings you closer to the vision you hold for your family's future. As you navigate this path, remember that you're not alone. Contact support networks or friends who share your commitment to positive change. Share experiences, learn from one another, and draw strength from knowing that many others are walking alongside you on this path.

Embrace your role as a cycle breaker with courage and compassion, knowing that every effort contributes to building a legacy of love, resilience, and hope for future generations. Celebrate each success—big or small—and continue moving forward with an open heart, ready to embrace whatever comes next.

Healing the Past: Rewriting Your Story

Understanding the power of narrative is like discovering the hidden chapters of your life story. These personal narratives, often written in childhood, profoundly impact how you view yourself and interact with the world. They color your perception, like a pair of tinted glasses you didn't know you were wearing. Perhaps you grew up hearing tales of your inadequacy, unintentionally passed down through generations. These stories are not just bedtime tales but scripts that influence behavior and relationships. They dictate how you react under stress, shaping interactions with your children. When you perceive yourself as inadequate, you may project that insecurity onto them, inadvertently stifling their growth.

Reframing personal stories becomes a journey toward healing and growth. It's about taking the pen into your hands and rewriting those tired, old scripts. One effective method involves writing exercises designed to transform negative narratives. Grab a notebook and reflect on a story from your past that still haunts you. Please write it down in vivid detail, then rewrite it with a positive twist, focusing on resilience and lessons learned. This exercise shifts your perspective and helps release the grip of past events. Seeking therapy can provide further insight into these narratives, offering a safe space to explore and rewrite personal stories with professional guidance. Therapists can help uncover underlying themes and offer tools to reframe them in a healthier light.

Forgiveness and letting go are pivotal in healing past wounds and rewriting family history. Forgiveness isn't about condoning past actions but freeing yourself from their hold. Practicing forgiveness exercises for both self and others can lighten emotional burdens. Picture yourself holding a balloon representing past grievances. Now imagine letting it go, watching it drift into the sky until it vanishes from sight. This symbolic release can be empowering, allowing space for new beginnings. Developing rituals to let go of past burdens can also be cleansing. Consider writing down grievances on paper, then burning them as a ritualistic release gesture.

Creating a new family story is the final step in this transformative process. Engage in storytelling activities with your children to foster a sense of shared history and connection. Gather around the dinner table or campfire, sharing tales emphasizing growth and resilience. These stories become the threads that weave your family's tapestry, highlighting lessons learned and triumphs celebrated. Documenting family achievements and lessons learned reinforces this narrative. Create a scrapbook or digital journal filled with photos, quotes, and reflections capturing moments of resilience and growth. This tangible record is a testament to your family's journey, reminding everyone that past narratives do not define you but by the strength to rewrite them.

In understanding the power of narrative, you realize that while you can't change the past, you can shape its impact on your present and future. Each step toward reframing personal stories brings healing and growth, allowing you to break free from the chains of old narratives that no longer serve you or your family. In this process, you foster an environment where love, understanding, and resilience thrive—where new stories can flourish without the weight of past burdens holding them back.

As you navigate this path, remember that rewriting your story isn't about erasing scars but embracing them as part of your unique journey. It's about acknowledging where you've been while choosing your next destination. With each rewritten chapter, you break free from limiting beliefs and create space for new narratives filled with hope, growth, and endless possibilities for yourself and future generations.

By embracing this process, you lay the foundation for a legacy rooted not in dysfunction but in strength—a legacy that honors the past while celebrating all that lies ahead on this incredible journey called life.

The Resilience Roadmap: Creating a New Legacy

Imagine building a house without a solid foundation. It might stand for a while, but eventually, it'll crumble. The same goes for resilience in families. Establishing core family values that promote resilience is like laying down the bricks and mortar that hold everything together. Think of values as the guiding principles that steer your family through life's choppy waters. They could be anything from honesty and kindness to perseverance and adaptability. Sit down with your family and brainstorm these values together. This gives everyone a voice and ensures that each member feels invested in maintaining them.

Consider creating a family mission statement once you've pinned down those values. This doesn't need to be a lengthy document; even a simple phrase can encapsulate what your family stands for. Maybe it's "We face challenges together" or "Kindness first." Display it somewhere visible, like the fridge door or a family bulletin board. This constant reminder is an anchor during turbulent times, reinforcing the resilience you're all working to cultivate.

Resilience isn't just something you talk about; it's something you practice. There are practical ways to build resilience in both parents and children. Teaching problem-solving skills through family challenges is one effective method. Have you ever tried planning a family vacation on a budget? It's a great way to involve everyone in decision-making and problem-solving. Encourage your kids to brainstorm solutions and weigh the pros and cons of each option. This teaches them critical thinking and reinforces the idea that challenges can be overcome.

Another strategy is to encourage adaptability and flexibility in family routines. Life is unpredictable, and clinging too rigidly to plans can lead to unnecessary stress. Teach your family to roll with the punches by occasionally switching things up—perhaps it's a spontaneous weekend trip or a surprise game night midweek. These changes help everyone learn to adapt and enjoy life's unexpected twists.

Modeling resilience for children is crucial because they often learn by watching us. Share personal stories of overcoming adversity, whether it's a tough day at work or a past challenge you've conquered. These narratives teach them that setbacks are not the end but growth opportunities.

Encourage your kids to take on age-appropriate challenges, whether learning a new skill or tackling a difficult homework project. Support them without hovering, allowing them to experience both the struggle and the triumph that follows.

Recognizing the journey of breaking cycles and building resilience is just as important as the destination itself. Host family gatherings to reflect on progress, where each person shares their achievements and lessons learned. It's like holding a mini-celebration for growth, acknowledging that every step toward resilience is worth celebrating.

Consider creating a family legacy book documenting this journey. Include photos, stories, and reflections from each member about their growth and the family's evolution. This tangible keepsake records your journey and is a powerful reminder of what you've accomplished together.

As we wrap up this chapter on building resilience, remember that it's not about never falling but about getting back up each time you do. It's about teaching your family that while life may throw curveballs, you have the strength and unity to catch them together.

Looking ahead, we'll explore how to shift priorities for your family. By fitting these insights into daily life, you'll continue forging an unbreakable bond rooted in love, understanding, and resilience.

REFLECTION JOURNAL PROMPTS

Take a deep breath....

These are just for you. There is no pressure to have the perfect answer—write what comes to mind.

"Identifying Patterns: The First Step to Change":

1. What recurring reactions or behaviors have you noticed in yourself, especially during stress or conflict?

2. Where do you think these patterns originated, and how have they served or limited you over time?

3. What would change in your life or relationships if you began responding differently the next time that pattern appeared?

"Conscious Parenting: Making Intentional Choices":

1. What does being a conscious parent mean to you, and how do you bring intention into your daily interactions with your child?

2. Can you recall when you paused to choose a mindful response instead of reacting automatically? What did that moment teach you?

3. What values or long-term goals guide your parenting decisions, even when the immediate situation feels overwhelming?

"Cycle Breaker: Embracing the Role of Change Agent":

1. What generational patterns or behaviors have you chosen to break, and what motivated you to make that decision?

2. How has stepping into the role of a cycle breaker impacted your sense of identity, purpose, or parenting style?
3. What challenges have you faced in breaking old cycles, and what strengths or supports have helped you stay committed to change?

"Healing the Past: Rewriting Your Story":
1. What past experiences still influence how you see yourself today, and how would you like to reframe those moments through a lens of compassion and growth?
2. If you could speak to your younger self during a painful time, what would you say to help them feel seen, safe, and supported?
3. How has acknowledging and working through your past shaped the narrative you choose to live and pass on to others?

"The Resilience Roadmap: Creating a New Legacy":
1. What does resilience mean to you, and how has your journey shaped that definition?

2. What values or lessons do you hope to pass down as part of the new legacy you're building for your family or community?

3. How have your struggles and triumphs equipped you to lead others, especially your children, through challenges with strength and hope?

CHAPTER 5

The Parenting Pivot: Shifting Priorities for Your Family

Imagine this: you're in a meeting dragging on longer than a Monday morning. Your phone buzzes with a text—a picture of your kid holding a ribbon from the school race you forgot about. It's a gut punch, reminding you of the juggling act we call life. This is where the parenting pivot comes into play. It's that moment when you realize something's gotta give, and it's usually not the family.

Recognizing an imbalance is like noticing your favorite pair of jeans getting tight. At first, you might ignore it, but eventually, it's hard to miss. Missing family events and constant work stress are signals that priorities need adjusting. The impact isn't just on you; it ripples through the family. Kids notice when you're absent or distracted, even if they don't say it out loud. It can create a disconnect, making family time feel more like a checkbox than a cherished moment.

Shifting priorities involves taking a hard look at what matters most. Start by creating a family vision board. Collect images and words that represent your family's goals and values. It's an engaging way to visualize what success looks like for your family unit. Alongside this, establish a priority list that includes family activities, no matter how small. Whether it's Sunday pancake breakfasts or Friday movie nights, having these on your list reminds you what you're working toward.

Aligning family and career goals might seem like trying to fit a square peg in a round hole, but it doesn't have to be. Look for opportunities to involve your family in career events. Bring your kids to work on family days or share your work projects with them in kid-friendly terms. This inclusion helps them understand what you do and why it matters. Consider career paths that support work-life harmony. Some companies offer flexible working hours or remote work options, freeing up more family time.

Implementing these changes requires actionable steps. Schedule regular family meetings to discuss priorities and check in on everyone's needs. It's like a mini-board meeting with more snacks and fewer spreadsheets. Use time management tools like shared calendars or apps to allocate time effectively. These tools help ensure that family commitments don't get lost in the chaos of everyday life.

Reflection Exercise

Take ten minutes at the end of each week to reflect on any moments of imbalance you experienced. Write down what triggered them and how they affected your family dynamics. Consider ways to address these issues moving forward. Regularly assessing your priorities and adjusting as needed will create a more harmonious balance between work and family life. Incorporating these strategies into daily life may seem like a tall order, but remember: small steps lead to significant change over time. Balancing work and family doesn't mean achieving perfection; it means finding harmony that works for everyone involved.

As fathers, we can model what it means to prioritize family while pursuing personal and professional goals. It's about showing up for our kids in person and commitment, demonstrating that they are valued and loved above all else.

So here's to embracing the parenting pivot with open arms— making those necessary shifts that bring us closer to our families while pursuing our passions outside the home.

Creating Time for Connection: Quality Over Quantity

It's easy to get caught up in the hustle, believing that more time equals better relationships. But let's face it, spending countless hours together doesn't always translate into meaningful connections. It's not about the clock; it's about the moments that matter. Quality time is like savoring a fine meal rather than eating a buffet. It's about focused, intentional engagement where you're fully present. Planning dedicated family nights can transform ordinary evenings into memorable occasions.

Imagine a movie night where everyone picks a film or a craft session with a theme—perhaps pirates or astronauts. This sparks creativity and strengthens bonds as everyone collaborates and participates.

One-on-one time with each child is equally precious. It's a chance to dive deep into their world to discover what makes them tick. Whether a simple walk around the block or a trip to their favorite ice cream shop, these personal adventures foster trust and understanding. You get to be their friend, the one who knows them best. This individualized attention shows them they're special and valued, reinforcing their self-esteem and sense of belonging.

Finding time can feel like squeezing juice from a rock in our fast-paced lives. But even limited moments hold potential for connection. Commute times offer golden opportunities for meaningful conversations. Turn off the radio and talk about the day ahead, or share silly stories from your childhood. These car chats become cherished rituals that break the monotony of daily routines. Incorporating small rituals into everyday life also works wonders. Bedtime stories aren't just for winding down; they're gateways to imagination and bonding. As you read together, you create shared experiences that linger long after turning the last page.

Choosing high-impact activities can elevate family time from mundane to memorable. Volunteering as a family builds empathy and teamwork while contributing to the community. Whether helping at a local food bank or participating in a neighborhood cleanup, these experiences instill values that last a lifetime. Another great option is family outings, which encourage teamwork, like escape rooms or obstacle courses. They challenge everyone to work together toward a common goal, strengthening family ties through collaboration and support.

Establishing family traditions is like planting seeds that blossom into cherished memories. Annual camping trips or similar adventures offer a break from routine, immersing everyone in nature's embrace. These excursions become stories you retell over campfires and dinners, binding you with shared memories. Weekly game nights or cooking sessions infuse joy into ordinary days, turning them into something special. As you roll the dice or stir pots together, laughter and friendship fill the air, creating bonds that withstand the test of time.

Reflection Section

Take a moment to reflect on your current family habits. Are there opportunities to create new traditions or enhance existing ones? Consider what activities resonate most with your family and how to incorporate them into your routine. Jot down ideas for themed family nights or one-on-one outings with each child. Keep this list handy as inspiration for future connections.

Connection isn't about perfection; it's about presence and intention. It's about making the most of what you have, no matter how small it may seem. By focusing on quality over quantity in your interactions, you build relationships rooted in love and understanding—relationships that thrive amidst life's chaos.

These moments become the fabric of your family story—the tales your children will carry with them as they grow. They're reminders that even in our busy lives, we can find time for what truly matters: each other.

So here's to prioritizing quality time with our families, embracing those small moments that make a big difference, and creating lasting connections that enrich our lives beyond measure.

Digital Detox: Reclaiming Family Time

Have you ever caught yourself scrolling through your phone, only to look up and realize the whole evening has slipped away? Maybe it's just me, but digital distractions have a knack for sneaking into our lives and quietly stealing precious moments. The constant ping of notifications, the allure of social media, and the endless stream of news can create a bubble that isolates us from those we care about most. These habits not only eat into family time but also affect relationships profoundly. We might be in the same room, yet miles apart emotionally. The psychological effects of always being "on" can lead to increased stress and decreased satisfaction in family interactions as our minds drift toward digital realms instead of staying present.

Implementing a digital detox plan can feel like trying to wrestle an octopus—so many tentacles of technology are gripping tightly. But it doesn't have to be daunting. Start by setting specific "no device" times during meals. Imagine dinner as a tech-free sanctuary where everyone gathers to share stories, not screens. These moments become islands of connection in the sea of digital chaos. Creating tech-free zones in the home can further reinforce this boundary. Designate specific areas like the living room or bedrooms as device-free havens where family members can engage with each other without distraction. These spaces encourage conversation and foster genuine interaction, turning them into nurturing environments for thriving relationships.

Encouraging offline activities is like opening a treasure chest filled with endless possibilities for family fun. Organizing outdoor excursions such as hiking or biking offers a chance to reconnect with nature while spending quality time together. It's incredible how a simple walk through the woods or a leisurely bike ride can spark conversations and laughter that might otherwise get lost in the digital noise. Hosting board game nights brings everyone together around the table, fostering friendly competition and collaboration. Whether it's an intense round of Monopoly or a lighthearted game of charades, these evenings create memories that stick, unlike fleeting digital interactions that vanish as quickly as they appear.

Balancing technology with family time doesn't mean banishing all devices; it's about finding harmony. Use apps designed to monitor and limit screen time, ensuring that technology enhances rather than detracts from life. Set reasonable boundaries that allow for necessary tech use without overwhelming family interactions. Encourage digital hobbies that involve the whole family, like photography or video-making projects. These activities blend creativity with technology, providing opportunities for collaboration and shared accomplishments.

Textual Element: Case Study

Consider one family: They struggled to connect amidst their busy schedules and growing screen time. They saw remarkable changes by implementing a weekly digital detox day—a Saturday without screens. They replaced screen time with family hikes, cooking experiments, and spontaneous dance-offs in the living room. This shift not only strengthened their bonds but also improved their overall well-being. This story illustrates how small changes can significantly enhance family dynamics.

Recognizing digital distractions and taking proactive steps to counter them is crucial for reclaiming valuable family time. It's about creating an environment where everyone feels seen and heard through pixels and genuine human interaction. By incorporating these strategies into daily life, you foster connections that endure beyond fleeting digital moments.

Ultimately, it's not about eliminating technology; it's about using it wisely to enhance rather than hinder family relationships. In doing so, you create a balance for meaningful connections in an increasingly wired world, where love and laughter take center stage over likes and follows.

As you embark on this digital detox journey with your family, remember that even small changes can make a big difference over time. Embrace opportunities for offline engagement and cherish those moments of genuine connection—they are the threads that weave together the fabric of family life.

In navigating the complexities of modern parenting amidst technological advances, let us strive for harmony between screen time and face time, for genuine connection flourishes in those face-to-face interactions.

Building a Support Network: Finding Your Dad Community

A solid support network is like having an emergency toolkit in your trunk. It's there when you need it, offering emotional support and shared experiences that make the load a little lighter. Imagine the relief of talking to someone who gets it—someone who's been in the trenches of parenthood and emerged with stories to tell and tips to share. A community of fellow dads can provide advice on everything from diaper disasters to teenage tantrums. It's not just about sharing the good times; it's about having a lifeline when things get tough. And let's face it, sometimes you need someone to nod knowingly while you vent about the mysterious stain you found on your couch.

But it doesn't stop there. A dad community can offer shared childcare and responsibilities opportunities, making those never-ending to-do lists less daunting. Whether swapping babysitting duties or organizing playdates, having a network means you don't have to go alone. Plus, there's something incredibly heartwarming about watching your kids form friendships with your friends' children, creating bonds that could last a lifetime.

Finding your community might initially seem daunting, but it's easier than you think. Start by exploring local parenting groups or meet-ups. Many communities have dad-focused groups that gather for coffee, playdates, or weekend barbecues. These gatherings are perfect for breaking the ice and finding like-minded fathers who share your interests and values. Online platforms can also be invaluable resources for connecting with other dads. Websites and forums dedicated to fatherhood provide spaces to share experiences, seek advice, and build friendships with fathers worldwide. The beauty of online communities is that they're accessible anytime, allowing you to engage in meaningful conversations even when life gets busy.

Once you've found your community, cultivating meaningful connections involves showing up and being involved. Regularly attending group activities or meetings helps strengthen those bonds and creates a sense of belonging within the community. Consider hosting social events for fellow fathers and their families to deepen connections. Whether it's a backyard barbecue or a family game night, these gatherings foster friendship and create opportunities for everyone to relax and enjoy each other's company.

Leverage this newfound network for personal and family growth by sharing parenting tips and resources. You never know when someone's advice might be the solution you've been searching for—or when your own experiences could help another dad in need. Collaborating on community service projects with other dads is another fantastic way to give back while building stronger ties within your group. It's a rewarding way to teach your children about empathy and kindness, all while working together towards a common goal.

Mindful Presence: Being There When It Counts

Being mindfully present with your family is similar to putting on a pair of noise-canceling headphones amidst the chaos of a bustling airport, where the disharmony of the outside world gradually dulls to a mere whisper, allowing you to immerse yourself fully and attentively in the present moment. This act of presence goes beyond mere physical proximity; it involves an emotional and mental engagement that enriches the family dynamic. Through this conscious and deliberate connection, we communicate to our families that they are of utmost significance, fostering an environment of love, respect, and appreciation. When such mindful presence is consistently practiced, it creates a profound ripple effect that deepens family bonds, cultivating an environment where individual members feel genuinely valued and thoroughly heard.

Engaging in straightforward yet impactful practices like daily meditation with family members can be incredibly beneficial in cultivating this precious sense of presence. Picture this: a family gathered in the cozy living room, perhaps seated comfortably on plush cushions, embracing a few moments of shared silence—it becomes a sacred ritual. Imagine the ambient lighting softly dimmed while a gentle, guided meditation voice ushers you into calmness, wrapping you in tranquility and setting a harmonious tone for the rest of the day. Such moments serve as grounding forces, anchoring the family's daily interactions in peace and promoting a collective sense of unity that threads through all activities.

Similarly, practicing mindful listening during conversations with family members can be revolutionary. Consider the act of truly listening, where the art of listening becomes an immersive experience. Imagine intently focusing on the words and emotions a loved one expresses without allowing your mind to wander or internal thoughts to interrupt. Picture the look of delight and relief on their face when they perceive that their words resonate with you, affirming that they are genuinely important to your world. This attentive presence, which conveys respect and validity to their feelings, builds layers of trust and deepens connections.

Balancing the demands of presence alongside other responsibilities in life can often feel as complex as juggling fiery torches while precariously balanced on a unicycle. Yet, thoughtful preparation and strategic planning can become a graceful juggling act. Begin by setting clear and defined boundaries that help define work from family time, creating a protective cocoon around your family interactions. Imagine dedicating specific hours to family, where the temptation to check work emails or notifications is deliberately muted, allowing you to be mentally and physically immersed in those vital family moments. This dedicated engagement fosters an atmosphere where every family member feels honored and significant, free from the infringements of work obligations.

Celebrating moments of connection with your family is similar to showering a cupcake with vibrant sprinkles—the small embellishments that inject sweetness and joy into daily existence. Capturing these precious family moments through photographs or journaling transforms them into a cherished archive. Visualize sitting together, flipping through photo albums with history, laughter-filled adventures, and shared triumphs, or imagine opening a gratitude jar brimming with daily notes of joy and gratitude. Over time, this collection becomes a source of happiness and cherished memories—concrete reminders of how love and laughter have been woven into the fabric of family life. Regularly revisiting these captured moments reinforces the profound significance of being present and cherishing each day together as a unit.

In conclusion, mindful presence transcends the simplistic notion of being physically present; it represents an intentional and heartfelt commitment to the well-being of those we love. By fostering an environment of intentionality and openness, we create a nurturing space where every family member feels deeply seen, acknowledged, and cherished amidst life's unavoidable chaos. As we diligently focus on cultivating this enriching presence, we metaphorically build structures of resilient and lasting relationships that thrive on profound connection, understanding, and empathy. Our journey now leads us to explore the distinctions of managing emotions within the family context, where embracing vulnerability strengthens, paving the way for overcoming societal stereotypes, and a more profound understanding.

REFLECTION JOURNAL PROMPTS

Take a deep breath....

These are just for you. There is no pressure to have the perfect answer—write what comes to mind.

"The Parenting Pivot: Shifting Priorities for Your Family":

1. What life event or realization prompted you to re-evaluate your parenting priorities, and how did it change your approach?
2. What priorities used to seem important that no longer serve your family's well-being, and what have you chosen to focus on instead?
3. How has shifting your parenting priorities influenced the connection, rhythm, or harmony within your home?

"Creating Time for Connection: Quality Over Quantity":

1. What small, meaningful moments have brought you closer to your child, even when time was limited?
2. How do you intentionally create space for connection in your daily routine, and what gets in the way?
3. In what ways has focusing on quality time over quantity shifted the emotional climate in your family?

"Digital Detox: Reclaiming Family Time":

1. How has screen time impacted how your family connects, and what signs told you it was time to change?

2. What challenges have you faced when reducing digital distractions, and how have you worked through them as a family?

3. What new routines, activities, or traditions have emerged from reclaiming screen-free time together?

"Building a Support Network: Finding Your Dad Community":

1. What does having a supportive community of other dads mean to you, and how has it shaped your parenting experience?

2. What barriers have you faced in seeking or building a dad community, and what helped you overcome them?

3. In what ways have other fathers challenged, inspired, or supported you on your journey through parenthood?

"Mindful Presence: Being There When It Counts":

1. When have you felt most present with your child, and what made that moment meaningful or memorable?

2. What distractions or habits tend to pull you away from being fully present, and how do you work to bring your attention back?

3. How has practicing mindful presence changed how your child responds to you emotionally or behaviorally?

CHAPTER 6

OVERCOMING SOCIETAL STEREOTYPES

Redefining Masculinity: Embracing the Nurturer Role

Picture this: you're in the middle of a bustling grocery store, toddler in one arm, a shopping list that's now more art than plan in the other. A fellow shopper gives you that look, suggesting you're slightly out of your depth as if nurturing isn't a man's domain. It's a moment that makes you pause and reflect on the expectations society has stacked upon us. Traditional masculinity has long been a fortress of indifference and emotional restraint, suggesting that real men don't show vulnerability or take on roles that are seen as nurturing. This stereotype demands that we be the sole providers, the rocks, the unemotional powerhouses. It's as if we're expected to operate as emotional robots simply because that's how it's always been. But let's be honest—this model is outdated and limiting.

The pressure to embody these ideals can weigh heavily on fatherhood roles. You're expected to be the breadwinner, the stoic leader who never flinches. But in reality, carrying the entire family's financial and emotional burden without allowing yourself to express vulnerability is exhausting. It's like trying to keep a ship afloat with just one oar. The expectation of constant strength can create a barrier between you and your children, where showing emotion is perceived as a weakness rather than authenticity.

Now, imagine shifting that narrative. Fathers embrace the nurturer role instead of being confined to rigid roles, sharing caregiving responsibilities equally with their partners. This isn't just about splitting chores—it's about genuinely engaging in those everyday moments that build connection. Think about it: bedtime stories that transport your children to far-off lands or the joy of cooking a family meal together, where flour ends everywhere but in the bowl. These nurturing activities aren't burdens; they're bonds waiting to be strengthened.

Embracing nurturing roles benefits not only you but your entire family. Sharing caregiving duties fosters a sense of partnership and teamwork at home, creating a balanced environment where everyone feels valued. It allows your partner to pursue their goals and passions while giving your children diverse role models who exemplify empathy and kindness. When fathers step into these roles, they demonstrate that masculinity isn't defined by toughness alone but by the capacity to love deeply and care sincerely.

Modeling emotional openness is another crucial aspect of redefining masculinity. Children learn more from what they see than what they're told. By openly sharing your emotions and experiences with your family, you create a safe space for them to do the same. It might feel awkward at first, like trying to dance at a wedding when you've got two left feet—but it gets easier with practice. Allow your children to see your struggles and triumphs so they understand that emotions are a regular part of life.

Encouraging children to express their feelings freely is essential to this process. Create an environment where they feel comfortable talking about their emotions without fear of judgment or dismissal. When they come to you upset about a scraped knee or a lost toy, listen empathetically and validate their feelings. This approach nurtures their emotional intelligence and strengthens their relationship with them. Redefining strength in this context means recognizing that true strength lies in being emotionally available and supportive. It's about shedding the armor society has told us to wear and embracing vulnerability as a source of power rather than weakness. Personal stories can beautifully illustrate this point. Think back to those moments when nurturing actions led to profound family connections—when comforting your child after a nightmare ended with both giggling over shared dreams, or helping with homework turned into an unplanned bonding session over math problems and hot cocoa. These moments reveal that nurturing isn't just beneficial; it's transformative.

Reflection Exercise

Reflect on your experiences with nurturing roles in your family life. Consider moments when stepping into this role felt natural or when you hesitated due to societal expectations. What barriers did you face? How did embracing these roles impact your relationship with your children? Use this reflection to explore what redefining masculinity means for you personally, embracing vulnerability as a strength rather than a burden. As we break free from conventional norms around masculinity and fatherhood roles, remember that change begins with each small step forward, like ripples spreading across still water until they transform into waves of lasting impact.

Vulnerability Hangover: Embracing Emotional Honesty

Picture this: you've just had a heartfelt conversation with someone dear to you, your partner, or your children. You've courageously peeled back the layers of your emotional armor, revealing the fears, hopes, and dreams that dwell within the depths of your soul. In the moment, there's a sense of liberation, a weight lifted from your chest. But shortly after comes what many have come to call the vulnerability hangover. After such openness leaves you mulling over whether you shared too much or bared your emotional core excessively, that unsettling feeling envelops you. This feeling is not a mere figment of your imagination but a tangible, palpable reaction to exposure. Your thoughts may race uncontrollably with apprehensions about being judged, being seen as weak, or failing to live up to the larger-than-life image society often imposes upon fathers as unshakeable pillars of strength.

Yet, here's an important realization: embracing this form of vulnerability is the birthplace of authentic connections. It's similar to acknowledging that you don't possess all the answers, which is perfectly acceptable. Recounting personal tales where I dared to lower my guard and was met with understanding rather than contempt has led to profound changes. For instance, I recall a moment when I confessed to my child that I was at a loss for an answer to a complex question about the workings of life. To my surprise, instead of spotting disappointment dancing in their eyes, I saw a glimmer of relief and empathy. This incident blossomed into a teaching moment for both of us—a gentle reminder that emotional honesty fosters growth and a deeper understanding within family bonds.

The advantages of embracing emotional honesty are truly multifaceted. Showing the cloak of judgment and fear and revealing your genuine self lays the groundwork for more profound and resilient family ties. Your children begin to perceive you not solely as an enforcer or provider but as a complicated, multidimensional individual navigating similar emotional waters. It's similar to peeling back the layers of an onion only to discover the rich complexity beneath—without the tears, of course.

Practically, incorporating vulnerability into parenting involves a series of deliberate actions. Initiating a journaling practice where you document your innermost feelings and encounters can be surprisingly therapeutic. While it may sound like an exercise ripped from a self-help manual, trust me, the simple act of committing emotions to paper can provide unexpected solace. Writing things down aids in processing and comprehending emotions. It's much like holding a private dialogue with oneself, a dialogue that remains shielded from external ears.

Additionally, fostering open dialogues with your partner regarding emotions can render vulnerability less intimidating and overwhelming. These exchanges don't require profound philosophical discourse; they demand sincerity. Converse about your thoughts, be it the anxieties you harbor regarding work or the joy resulting from minor victories. Engaging in such discussions usually can ease the path for more open communication with your children, vividly illustrating that emotions are not to be smothered but expressed freely. Establishing an atmosphere where vulnerability is championed starts with creating a culture of openness and acceptance. Initiate family gatherings where discussions about emotions and challenges are tolerated and actively welcomed. These meetings form a sanctuary where all family members feel safe to unburden their minds and hearts with neither fear of criticism nor ridicule. Children, in particular, thrive in such environments, quickly learning that their voices carry weight and their feelings hold validity.

Encourage your kids to articulate their fears and uncertainties. What may seem trivial to adults might be of monumental significance in their universe—a missing toy, a challenging day at school, or perhaps a disagreement with a friend.

Demonstrate to them that voicing these matters is not merely permissible but appreciated. This seemingly small gesture nurtures resilience and bolsters their confidence in navigating life's undulating journey.

Remember, vulnerability isn't a trait we naturally drift toward—it's more like an unwelcomed guest that lingers longer than anticipated—but it is indispensable in forging genuine bonds. The path to emotional honesty may initially appear daunting, yet it promises relationships founded on mutual admiration and empathy.

As you tread this parenting path, give yourself the grace to err and hesitate. Sometimes, vulnerability feels like traversing a minefield rather than a peaceful path, but that establishes part of the journey. Each endeavor toward embracing emotional honesty enriches not only your life but the lives of those in your neighborhood.

By inviting vulnerability into our lives, we instill in our children that to be human is to embrace the full spectrum of emotions without the burden of shame or fear and that genuine strength resides in openness and authenticity with oneself and others.

In this shared voyage toward deeper bonds formed through vulnerability, let us acknowledge and celebrate every small triumph—a candid conversation here, an honest acknowledgment there—as vital milestones on our quest to build more robust family connections anchored in love and understanding.

Breaking Free from Conventional Norms

Imagine this: you're sitting at your desk, eyes glazed over as you try to focus on the spreadsheet that seems to grow with every glance. Your phone buzzes with a picture of your kid holding up a drawing they made just for you, face beaming with pride. And yet, you're stuck in the office, missing another moment in the name of providing. Society has long painted this picture of fatherhood as synonymous with work, where climbing the career ladder takes precedence over family dinners and bedtime stories. The expectation is that fathers should prioritize work, always putting the bread on the table above all else. But who says it has to be like this? This norm creates a gap between personal growth and family connection, where the heart and home are sidelined in pursuit of success. Traditional norms also dictate that fathers should be disciplinarians rather than nurturers, tolerant rule enforcers who keep emotions tucked away. It's like living life with only one tool in a toolbox. A hammer is useful, but try fixing a leaky pipe with it. This expectation smothers your opportunity to connect with your children on a deeper level and limits your growth as a parent. You miss those tender moments where vulnerability and understanding can transform relationships. So, how do we break these chains? It starts with reevaluating personal beliefs. Take some time to reflect on the values you hold dear and where they come from. Do they align with the kind of parent you want to be? Often, we inherit beliefs from our upbringing, carrying them like family heirlooms without considering if they still fit our lives. Identifying those that no longer serve your family dynamic is crucial. It may be time to retire the notion that fathers should be detached authority figures or that work must always come first. Challenging these outdated beliefs paves the way for more authentic parenting. Engaging in discussions with peers about non-traditional parenting roles can be enlightening. It's like getting fresh eyes on a problem you've been staring at for too long. Hearing how others navigate similar challenges offers new perspectives and reinforces that you're not alone in wanting something different. Experimenting with new family routines can also help break free from norms. Try swapping roles or introducing activities that challenge traditional dynamics. Maybe you take charge of school pick-ups while your partner handles dinner—simple shifts that send a powerful message about equality and flexibility.

Celebrating uniqueness in fatherhood is about recognizing that there's no one-size-fits-all approach to parenting. It's okay to color outside the lines. Document unconventional family achievements and share stories of successful non-traditional parenting moments. These memories build a tapestry of love and connection—a testament to your unique style as a father. Whether hosting a backyard campout or leading a family art project, these experiences become treasured milestones. Parenting isn't a competition but an opportunity to create something beautiful and distinct within your family. Celebrate the diversity your approach brings by embracing what sets you apart from traditional norms. Let each unique choice be a reminder that fatherhood is as diverse as it is rewarding. Unconventional parenting isn't just about what you do differently; it's about how those differences enrich your family life. It's about finding joy in the journey (there's that word again!) of discovering what works best for your family, even if it doesn't fit into society's mold. When you break free from conventional norms, you permit yourself to explore new territories where love and connection thrive.

Imagine looking back on your life as a parent and seeing an assortment filled with vibrant colors and textures—all representing moments when you dared to step away from tradition and embrace what truly matters: being present for your family in ways that resonate with who you are at your core.

As we continue navigating this path together, remember that breaking free from conventional norms isn't about rejecting tradition entirely; it's about reshaping those traditions into something meaningful for you and your loved ones. Continue challenging those expectations that no longer serve you and embrace opportunities for growth along this remarkable journey of fatherhood.

And if ever in doubt, remember: there's no manual for parenting—only guidelines we choose to follow or rewrite as we see fit. Embrace this freedom wholeheartedly and celebrate all the unique ways it enriches your life as a father, one unconventional step at a time.

Progressive Fatherhood: Championing Equality in Parenting

Imagine standing in a room filled with the sweet echoes of children's laughter, where toys are scattered like colorful confetti, and the comforting scent of something delicious wafts in from the kitchen. This lively scene isn't a difference or a special occasion event, but a heartfelt glimpse into a family's everyday enthusiasm that embodies the principles of progressive fatherhood. This modern approach to fathering is precisely crafted on the steadfast principles of equality and shared responsibilities. It positions parenting as an experience that transcends mere role assignments dictated by tradition, transforming it into a collective and fulfilling family endeavor. The compelling concept of progressive fatherhood is revolutionizing how society perceives parenting roles by highlighting the critical importance of active involvement from both parents. It's grounded in the unwavering commitment to equal parenting duties. It portrays fathers as integral players who are just as involved in the myriad of day-to-day parenting activities—from diaper changes and school runs to bedtime stories and PTA meetings. This philosophy is a collective family effort that embraces the diversity in family dynamics and parenting roles, whether it signifies single dads, stay-at-home dads, or co-parenting arrangements that diverge from traditional practices.

In the honorable pursuit of promoting equality within the household, fathers have a unique opportunity to reshape social narratives around traditional roles. It begins with knowingly sharing household tasks and the multifaceted responsibilities of child-rearing equally and intentionally. Envision a typical evening: rather than one parent completely handling bath time while the other tends to catch up on work emails, both parents are genuinely involved in the nightly routine—a harmonious snap of comforting storybooks and soothing songs. This approach to separating labor eases individual burdens and strengthens the family by fostering a spirit of togetherness and teamwork. Encouragingly open and honest discussions about ingrained gender roles and expectations hold equal significance. These conversations can gracefully unfold around something as simple as the dinner table, encouraging family members to question why specific chores and responsibilities are traditionally assigned to one gender. Engaging children and all family members in such explorations of how these roles can be more equitably shared is crucial. It's about debunking long-held myths that specific household or parenting tasks are inherently suited to one gender over another. When fathers actively prompt and participate in these dialogues, they set a powerful example for their children, modeling a world where equality transforms from a mere abstract concept into a tangible, lived reality.

Community Engagement in Progressive Fatherhood

Fathers also possess the powerful capacity to become active advocates for gender equality within their broader communities. By engaging in parenting groups dedicated to championing equality, they become contributors to a wider, ongoing dialogue about parenting as a shared and inclusive endeavor. These groups provide critical platforms for exchanging innovative ideas and strategies, offering valuable support and friendship to those daring to challenge traditional norms. Furthermore, volunteering for community initiatives that promote inclusive parenting practices helps extend the scope of this advocacy. Whether it involves organizing community events, delivering workshops, or actively participating in campaigns that champion equitable parental leave policies for all genders, fathers possess the influential potential to catalyze societal change. This kind of active involvement sends a powerful, resonant message: equality in parenting isn't just beneficial for families—it's fundamentally necessary for the holistic growth of society.

Lasting Impacts of Equality on Family Dynamics

The impact of embracing equality on family dynamics is both profound and far-reaching. Children raised within such enriching environments tend to develop a balanced and open-minded view of gender roles. They grow up witnessing both parents engaging equally in various tasks—cooking meals, fixing bikes, and attending school events—leading them to understand that skills and capabilities are dictated not by gender but by personal interest and ability. Such exposure fosters respect and empathy, essential qualities serving them well as they navigate life's countless paths. Moreover, shared experiences and responsibilities help build unbreakable family bonds. When fathers engage deeply and actively in parenting, they promote profound, meaningful connections with their children, creating cherished memories that aren't tied solely to special occasions but are beautifully interwoven into the fabric of everyday life. These shared moments, whether they encompass building towering pillow forts or delving into exciting science projects together, become the threads that form a strong, resilient family tapestry.

As we draw this chapter to a reflective close, it's evident that progressive fatherhood represents more than just a shift in societal roles; it's a transformative movement toward fostering a more inclusive and equitable future for all families. By embracing equality in parenting, fathers enhance their lives with richer relationships and experiences and pave the way for future generations to flourish in a world where both parents have the freedom and opportunity to participate equally in the joys and responsibilities of family life.

This chapter delves deeply into how progressive fatherhood champions equality and shared responsibilities, reshaping family dynamics meaningfully. As we transition to the next chapter, we will explore practical strategies for Emotional Healing within our families and build upon these foundational principles. Approaching your inner child with compassion is key to healing.

REFLECTION JOURNAL PROMPTS

Take a deep breath....

These are just for you. There is no pressure to have the perfect answer—write what comes to mind.

"Redefining Masculinity: Embracing the Nurturer Role":

1. What messages did you receive growing up about what it means to be a man, and how have they influenced your parenting approach?

2. When have you felt most connected to your nurturing side, and how did those around you receive that experience?

3. How are you intentionally redefining masculinity for yourself and modeling a broader, more compassionate version of fatherhood for your children?

"Vulnerability Hangover: Embracing Emotional Honesty":

1. Have you ever shared something deeply personal and later questioned whether it was "too much"? What did that experience teach you about emotional honesty?

2. What fears or insecurities arise after being emotionally open, and how do you work through them compassionately?

3. How has choosing to be emotionally honest, even when uncomfortable, transformed your relationships or sense of self?

"Breaking Free from Conventional Norms":

1. What societal or cultural expectations have you felt pressured to follow, and how have they conflicted with your personal values or parenting style?

2. Can you recall when choosing a different path outside the norm led to greater authenticity or connection in your family?

3. How are you intentionally redefining success, masculinity, or family roles to create a life that feels true to who you are?

"Progressive Fatherhood: Championing Equality in Parenting":

1. What does equal parenting mean to you, and how do you actively work to share responsibilities and emotional labor at home?

2. How have your views on fatherhood evolved, especially concerning gender roles and societal expectations?

3. What impact do you hope your approach to fatherhood will have on your children's understanding of equality and partnership?

"Community Engagement in Progressive Fatherhood":

1. How has being part of a broader community, local or online, shaped your journey as a progressive father?

2. In what ways do you contribute to building a more inclusive and supportive parenting culture in your community?

3. What does leadership in fatherhood look like to you, and how do you use your voice or actions to influence change beyond your household?

CHAPTER 7

TECHNIQUES FOR EMOTIONAL HEALING

Coping with Past Traumas: Facing Your Inner Child

Imagine this: you're at a family gathering, and out of nowhere, a seemingly harmless comment from a family member sends you spiraling back to your childhood. It's like being transported through time, where old feelings resurface, influencing your reactions today. This is where the concept of the inner child steps in—a pivotal player in the landscape of emotional healing. The inner child is not some mythical creature lurking in your psyche but rather a source of emotions and experiences from your formative years. It holds the joys, fears, and wounds of your past, shaping how you interact with the world now.

Understanding this inner child is crucial for healing past traumas. It's like unlocking a door to a room full of old memories, some cherished and others you'd rather forget. These childhood traumas often cast long shadows, influencing present behaviors in ways we might not immediately recognize. For instance, a fear of abandonment from childhood could manifest as clinginess in adult relationships. When you identify triggers linked to these early experiences, you start to see patterns that may have been invisible before. Recognizing these influences allows you to break free from their grip, offering a path toward healthier relationships and self-understanding. Consider practical exercises that foster connection and healing to engage with your inner child. Visualization exercises can be powerful here. Find a quiet space, close your eyes, and picture yourself meeting your younger self in a safe, comforting environment. Imagine offering them the love and reassurance they might have lacked. It's like giving a hug through time, mending those old wounds. Writing letters to your inner child is another effective technique. Pour your thoughts, express love and understanding, and validate their feelings. It's a cleansing process that bridges the gap between past and present. Approaching your inner child with compassion is key to healing. Think of it as offering a warm embrace to a part of yourself that has been overlooked for too long. Practicing self-compassion exercises helps in this endeavor. When self-critical, pause and replace those thoughts with words of kindness and encouragement. Affirmations can transform your mindset, creating a nurturing environment for emotional exploration. This approach fosters healing and builds resilience, allowing you to face future challenges with newfound strength.

Visualization Exercise: Comforting Your Inner Child

Find a comfortable spot where you won't be disturbed for a few minutes. Close your eyes and take a few deep breaths to center yourself. Picture yourself as a child in a safe, loving place— perhaps your childhood bedroom or a sunny park. Imagine approaching this younger version of yourself with warmth and kindness. What do they need to hear from you? What reassurance can you offer? Spend time in this mental space, offering comfort and understanding to your inner child.

Creating an environment favorable to emotional exploration involves more than self-examination; it also requires action. Set aside dedicated time for these practices, integrating them into your routine like any other self-care activity. Whether through journaling or engaging with support groups, prioritize this healing journey as an essential part of your life.

Engaging with the inner child is not about dwelling on the past but about understanding it enough to move forward without its weight dragging you back. It's about recognizing that those early experiences shape you, but don't define who you can become. Embrace this process with patience and empathy for yourself—after all, we're all just trying to figure things out, one step at a time.

As you use these techniques for emotional healing, remember that progress isn't linear; it's more like a winding road with unexpected detours and scenic viewpoints. Each effort counts toward creating a more resilient and compassionate version of yourself—one who embraces the past and future with open arms.

Nurturing your inner child through these practices will pave the way for healthier relationships and greater self-awareness in everyday life—a gift for yourself and everyone around you.

Strategies for Emotional Resilience: Building Inner Strength

Emotional resilience—those two words carry the weight of a life well-lived. It's the ability to bounce back from life's curveballs without crumbling like a soggy cereal box. Think of it as your emotional trampoline, helping you rebound when things get tough. It's about having the inner strength to navigate life's storms and come out with your sails intact. In personal and family life, resilience isn't just a luxury; it's a necessity. It lays the foundation for healthy relationships, where understanding and empathy thrive. Without resilience, the most minor setback can feel like a mountain, but with it, even the most significant hurdles become manageable.

Now, what forms the backbone of emotional resilience? It starts with calming a positive mindset. This isn't about plastering a smile on your face and pretending everything's fine when it's not. It's about seeing possibilities where others see problems. That little voice inside reminds you that every cloud has a silver lining, even if you have to squint to see it. Alongside positivity comes adaptability—the ability to roll with the punches and pivot gracefully when life throws you a curveball. It's like learning to dance in the rain rather than waiting for the storm to pass.

How do you build this resilience? Daily gratitude practice is a great start. It shifts your focus from what's lacking to what's abundant. Each morning, jot down three things you're grateful for, no matter how small. The aroma of freshly brewed coffee or a hug from your kid lingers longer than usual. This simple act rewires your brain to notice the good amidst the chaos. Engage in activities that promote mental and emotional flexibility, too. Try yoga or meditation—practices that teach you to bend without breaking, like a willow in the wind.

To measure growth in resilience, reflect on past challenges and how you handled them. Did you crumble under pressure or rise to the occasion? Seek feedback from family and peers as well. They often see the progress we're too close to notice ourselves. Ask them about changes they've observed in your ability to cope with stress. Their insights can be more enlightening than a thousand self-help books.

Journaling serves as another tool for tracking resilience growth. Please keep a record of trials and how you've overcome them. Over time, those pages will reveal patterns of strength and perseverance you might not have recognized. This reflection boosts your confidence and reminds you that you've weathered storms and can do so again.

Incorporating resilience-building strategies into daily life isn't just about ticking boxes on a checklist. It's about integrating these practices into the fabric of your existence, making them as routine as brushing your teeth or having that first cup of coffee in the morning. Create rituals reinforcing resilience, like family meetings where everyone shares the week's challenges and triumphs. These gatherings foster community and support while reinforcing that setbacks are just setups for comebacks. Remember, building emotional resilience is not an overnight task. It requires patience, persistence, and an open heart willing to learn from every experience, good or bad. It's about embracing life's unpredictability with a sense of humor and curiosity rather than fear or frustration.

So here's to building inner strength—one day at a time, one challenge at a time—creating lives filled with joy, connection, and resilience. Whether finding beauty in simplicity or navigating complexities with grace, remember that each step forward is progress worth celebrating.

The Power of Reflection: Journaling as a Healing Tool

Journaling offers a sanctuary for your thoughts, where you can spill your emotions without judgment. Imagine it as a private conversation with yourself, where honesty flows freely. When life throws curveballs, writing provides solace. It's not just about documenting events; it's about exploring your emotions. Putting pen to paper can release repressed feelings you didn't even realize you were holding onto. Think of it as emotional spring cleaning, clearing the clutter to make room for clarity and understanding. As you write, you unravel the tangled threads of your thoughts, finding patterns and insights that elude you in the chaos of everyday life.

Different journaling techniques cater to various emotional needs. Free writing is like opening the floodgates of your mind, allowing spontaneous thoughts to flow without restraint. It's liberating—no rules, no grammar police, just pure expression. Guided journaling prompts offer direction for those who crave a bit more structure. These prompts focus on specific emotional themes, encouraging deeper reflection. They might ask you to explore gratitude or confront fears you've been avoiding. Both methods serve as tools for self-discovery, helping you navigate the maze of your emotions with newfound awareness.

To make journaling a regular practice, consider setting aside a specific time each day to write. It could be in the morning when your mind is fresh or at night when you're winding down. Consistency is key. This routine transforms journaling from an occasional activity into a daily ritual that grounds you. Create a comfortable space dedicated to this reflection—perhaps a cozy nook with soft lighting and your favorite pen. This environment signals to your mind that it's time to unwind and connect with your inner world.

Journaling isn't just about venting; it's a tool for tracking progress on your emotional journey. Regularly reviewing past entries can be enlightening. You might notice recurring themes or patterns, offering insight into areas where growth has occurred or attention is still needed. Reflective questions guide this assessment: "What challenges have I faced recently? How did I handle them?" These questions encourage self-examination and highlight milestones achieved along the way. Over time, these entries become a testament to your resilience—a written record of how far you've come and where you're headed.

Journaling Prompt: Exploring Emotional Milestones

Set aside some quiet time to reflect on recent emotional experiences. Write about a challenge you faced and how you responded. What did you learn from the experience? How have you grown since then? Use these reflections as a compass to guide future decisions.

As you integrate journaling into your life, remember that perfection isn't the goal; authenticity is. Permit yourself to write without fear of judgment or expectation. Embrace the messiness of your emotions—let them spill onto the page unfiltered and raw. You create a space where healing can flourish—a safe harbor amidst life's storms.

Over time, this practice becomes more than just an outlet; it becomes a companion on your path to self-discovery. It offers solace during difficult times and celebrates victories—big or small—along the way. And while it may not solve all problems overnight, it provides something invaluable: perspective.

So grab that pen, find your favorite spot, and let the words flow. Whether pouring out frustrations or capturing moments of joy, each entry is a step toward greater understanding and acceptance of yourself and the world around you.

Seeking Support: Professional Help and Peer Groups

Despite our best efforts, we sometimes find ourselves stuck in emotional ruts that self-help books and late-night contemplation can't quite fix. That's when it becomes crucial to recognize the need for external support. This isn't about admitting defeat but acknowledging that other perspectives can illuminate paths we can't see ourselves. It's like having a guide who knows the terrain, helping you navigate the tricky parts of your emotional landscape. Understanding when self-help tools fall short is a strength, not a weakness. It's the realization that growth sometimes requires a team effort, and reaching out for help is a sign of courage and wisdom.

Professional help is valuable for those ready to dive deeper into emotional healing. Therapists, like the emotional mechanics they are, offer various tools tailored to your needs. Cognitive-behavioral therapy (CBT) helps rewire thought patterns that keep you spinning in circles. It's all about identifying and replacing those pesky negative thoughts with healthier ones. Psychotherapy digs deeper, exploring the root causes of emotional distress. It's like peeling back layers of an onion, uncovering the core issues that have been buried far too long. Counseling provides a safe space to address deep-seated emotional concerns without judgment, offering guidance and support through life's ups and downs.

Peer support groups offer another avenue for healing, creating a community where shared experiences foster understanding and connection. Imagine a room filled with people who get it—

no need to explain or justify your feelings because they've been there, too. These groups provide more than just sympathy; they offer accountability and motivation. You're more likely to stay committed to the process when you're part of a group striving toward similar goals. It's like having workout buddies for your emotional health, cheering you on when the going gets tough. Choosing the right support system can feel overwhelming, but some research can go a long way. When evaluating therapists, consider their credentials and areas of expertise. Compatibility matters, too; you want someone who resonates with your values and approach to healing. When I was recommended an EMDR therapist, trust is the key for both parties, so don't hesitate to ask questions or schedule initial consultations to find the right fit. Look for peer groups tailored to fathers or specific challenges you're facing. Whether online or in-person, these groups should feel welcoming and supportive, like a second home where you can share openly.

In this digital age, online resources abound, making finding support that suits your lifestyle easier than ever. Virtual therapy sessions offer flexibility for those juggling busy schedules, while online support groups provide anonymity for those who prefer privacy. The key is finding what works for you—something that fits seamlessly into your life without adding stress or strain.

Remember that seeking support isn't about fixing what's broken but enhancing what's already there. It's about building a resource network that strengthens your emotional resilience and enriches your life experiences. Everyone's path is unique, and there's no one-size-fits-all solution. Embrace the journey with an open heart and mind, knowing you're taking steps toward greater self-awareness and fulfillment.

As you explore these options, remember that growth takes time and patience. Be gentle with yourself as you navigate this process—stumbling along the way is okay. The important thing is that you're moving forward, seeking the support you need to thrive emotionally and personally.

Connecting with others who understand your struggles is incredibly powerful—it's like finding a lifeline when you're adrift at sea. Whether through professional help or peer groups, these connections remind you that you're not alone on this journey. They offer hope, encouragement, and reassurance that healing is possible and worthwhile.

So, take that first step toward seeking support with confidence and courage. Know that reaching out doesn't diminish your strength; it amplifies it by opening doors to new possibilities for growth and healing.

Emotional Healing Tailored for Fathers

Fathers, let's take a moment to acknowledge something important: the world often paints us as superheroes capable of handling any situation with unyielding strength and unwavering resolve. This societal portrait isn't just a simple expectation; it resembles a well-worn script handed down through generations, urging us to seamlessly balance the rigors of being steadfast providers and nurturing parents. At times, it may feel like we're asked to juggle flaming torches while precariously balanced on a unicycle, a metaphor for the juggling act of life's myriad responsibilities. These societal expectations cultivate a unique and diverse set of emotional challenges that often go unacknowledged. Picture carrying a heavy backpack labeled "Traditional Masculinity" as you climb Everest, symbolizing the enormous expectations placed on fathers to meet external demands while addressing their personal emotional needs. Yet, remember, you are not alone in scaling this difficult peak. Many fathers chart similar paths, striving to embody both the unyielding rock and the beating heart of their families, aiming to support and nurture all while maintaining composure.

Additionally, weaving emotional healing into your parenting role can lead to a transformative shift in family dynamics. Sharing insights from your emotional growth journey with your children holds remarkable power. It's similar to pulling back the curtain, granting them a glimpse of the reality that even superheroes experience moments of vulnerability. By modeling healthy emotional behaviors, you become a living testament that feeling deeply and articulating emotions is an integral part of the human experience. This openness fosters an environment where emotions are not concealed but validated, nurturing empathy and understanding within the family unit and sowing the seeds for emotional intelligence in children. Recognize and celebrate your journey toward emotional healing—it's not something to casually dismiss as trivial.

Acknowledging milestones on this journey underscores the effort and dedication invested in your growth. Consider establishing personal rituals to celebrate these accomplishments, whether it's a quiet moment of self-examination or treating yourself to a small reward upon reaching a personal goal. Sharing your success stories with peers or support groups can bolster this sense of achievement, transforming your journey into an inspiring beacon for others. It's like declaring, "So can you." These stories, instilled with your triumphs, inspire others, serving as tangible reminders of how far you've come on this path of emotional resilience. Emotional healing openly tailored for fathers isn't about reinventing the well-known wheel but refining it to suit your unique needs and circumstances. Whether attending insightful workshops or candidly sharing newfound wisdom with your family, each stride contributes to a calmer, healthier emotional landscape. As you continue navigating this healing chapter, honor your progress and openly share your journey with others, transforming personal growth into a shared experience. In the grand scheme of things, embracing emotional healing does more than enrich your personal life; it reverberates outward, profoundly impacting those around you. It creates positive change that extends beyond your immediate family, potentially influencing broader community dynamics and reshaping societal norms. As we delve further into the next chapter, consider how these insights can further enhance your dual role as provider and nurturer. Explore how healing practices, mindful moments, are elegantly woven into the fabric of daily life, creating a complex tapestry of resilience, connection, and enduring strength.

"If you or someone you know is struggling, please reach out for support. Contact Lifeline or a trusted mental health organization—you're not alone, and help is always available."

REFLECTION JOURNAL PROMPTS

Take a deep breath....

These are just for you. There is no pressure to have the perfect answer—write what comes to mind.

"Coping with Past Traumas: Facing Your Inner Child":

1. What memories or feelings from your childhood still surface in your parenting or personal life, and how do you respond to them?
2. If you could sit with your younger self during a painful moment, what would you want them to hear, feel, or know?
3. How has acknowledging and nurturing your inner child helped you break cycles or be more fully present for your children?

"Strategies for Emotional Resilience: Building Inner Strength":

1. What personal habits or practices help you stay grounded and emotionally steady during stress or uncertainty?
2. Can you recall a challenging situation that revealed your resilience? What did you learn about your capacity to cope and grow?
3. How do you model emotional strength and flexibility for your children, and what impact do you hope it has on their development?

"Seeking Support: Professional Help and Peer Groups":

1. What beliefs or fears have shaped your willingness to seek professional help or lean on others during difficult times?

2. How has connecting with peer groups or mental health professionals influenced your growth or parenting journey?

3. What kind of support feels most meaningful to you, and how might you take the first step toward accessing it?

"Emotional Healing Tailored for Fathers":

1. What emotional wounds or past experiences have you found yourself carrying into fatherhood, and how have they shaped how you parent?

2. What does healing look like for you as a father, and how do you create space for that process in your daily life?

3. How have your efforts to heal emotionally influenced your connection with your children, partner, or community?

CHAPTER 8

MINDFULNESS AND STRESS-REDUCTION

Mindful Moments: Finding Peace in Everyday Chaos

Ah, the familiar whirlwind of daily life, suggestive of an enthusiastically chaotic circus rehearsal where roles merge and blur—you could be the juggler fumbling with an array of unmanageable tasks or perhaps the clown, adorning a smile amid the mayhem. It's a vivid scene where breakfast spills merge seamlessly with urgent work emails while a toddler's tantrum creates a unique symphony. Imagine living this perpetual circus day in, day out. The quest for peace often seems like chasing a subtle unicorn through these bustling grounds, but it's well within reach, waiting quietly amid the turmoil. Introducing mindful moments, these cherished strongholds of tranquility are not the mythical sanctuaries of mountain retreats, which indeed hold their allure, but instead, they are practical nuggets of serenity discreetly nestled within your routine, like undiscovered Easter eggs. Mindful moments encompass simple, deliberate practices rooted in ushering conscious awareness to the present, promising to infuse calmness into your vibrant life tapestry.

Picture this ordinary occurrence: washing your hands. While it might seem routine, like brushing crumbs off a countertop, it harbors potential for mindfulness. Engage in this task with full attention—note each facet of the experience. Feel the varied temperatures as water caresses your skin, the tactile quality of soap, or its fragrant bouquet enveloping your senses. Such understated activities possess an inherent grounding power, anchoring you amid turbulent thoughts to the here and now. Imagine extending this mindfulness to your solitary morning stroll—the rare, precious moments belonging solely to you before the day's whirlwind ensues. During this sacred time, relinquish distractions and immerse in the sensory orchestra: the avian symphony overhead, the gentle whisper of leaves, and the subdued urban hum echoing in the distance. Absorb the chaos; don't merely acknowledge it but welcome it without judgment.

Infusing mindfulness into everyday tasks is similar to enriching a recipe with a dash of salt—it elevates and transforms the flavors of your entire day. Consider your dining habits. Instead of rushing through breakfast like a speed-eating competitor on a frenzied game show, engage deeply with each morsel. Dissect and savor the array of flavors and textures, perhaps even indulge in the unfamiliar experience of tasting your meal. This principle extends to listening, particularly within the family dynamic. By practicing mindful listening—entirely focusing on your children's words without creating the following grocery list in the recesses of your mind—you offer them a profound gift of presence. These rituals don't just convert mundane tasks into experiences; they enrich them.

The palpable benefits resulting from mindfulness stretch far beyond mere moments of calm. Picture your mind enjoying a luxurious spa day with enhanced mental clarity and emotional revitalization. Your focus, liberated from stress's clutches and the relentless pulls of anxiety, sharpens dramatically during parenting duties. And as for those overwhelming emotional waves threatening to overwhelm you during bustling days? These short-lived disturbances gradually lose their formidable strength as you learn to secure peace in the present. Mindful moments aren't about erasing life's challenges; they foster a heroic mindset, allowing you to approach obstacles with reinvigorated perspective and robustness.

To cultivate an environment conducive to mindfulness, evaluate practical adjustments at home. Begin decluttering spaces; unneeded distractions often steal your tranquility. A clean environment, almost magically, simplifies mental processes—I mean, locating that mysteriously subtle sock to complete your child's preferred footwear becomes unexpectedly straightforward. Elevate the atmosphere with calming aromas like lavender or chamomile; fragrant whispers transform ordinary rooms into tranquil sanctuaries amid the disharmony.

Reflection Exercise

Envision dedicating five minutes each morning to identify one daily task in which you intentionally practice mindfulness. Consistently use a journal to capture your observations, delving into shifts in awareness and emotional well-being. This exercise initiates a silent dialogue with yourself, fostering internal insights about how mindfulness transcends mere rituals and impacts daily life on a profound level.

Sure, amidst the layered complexities of your schedule, this proposition might seem idyllic yet overconfident. The essential beauty of mindful moments resides in their effortless integration into existing routines; they require no extra innings of time on your part. They're an invitation to enhanced presence and being, not to increased doing. Subtly introduce these moments to your daily life, weaving consistency and peace into your routine fabric with harmonious variability. While mindfulness doesn't wield magic wands capable of resolving every parenting trial, nor does it inspire immediate toddler slumbers or chore completion, it provides essential tools. It enables grace and resilience to navigate life's inevitable messiness. Raise a toast to discovering tranquility in chaos— one mindful moment at your own pace!

Guided Meditation: A Father's Path to Calm

Imagine you're in the middle of a chaotic day. The kids are arguing over who gets the remote, the dog is barking at an invisible threat, and your phone won't stop buzzing. Moments like these, that guided meditation swoops in like a trusty superhero. Guided meditation is like having a calm friend in your ear, gently leading you through a serene mental landscape. You don't need to be a meditation guru or live in a monastery to enjoy its benefits. With a calming voice guiding you, it's like someone holding your hand through the peaceful parts of your brain, inviting you to leave the chaos outside for a few precious minutes.

Apps like Headspace or Calm can be beneficial for those new to meditation. They offer sessions designed for beginners to ease you into the practice without feeling overwhelmed. It's as simple as choosing a session, plugging in your headphones, and listening. The guide's voice helps you focus on being present, moving away from stress and toward tranquility. Whether in your living room or sneaking a moment of peace in your car, guided meditation can become a refuge from the storm.

The benefits of regular meditation practice are profound and wide-ranging. Over time, it helps improve emotional regulation, allowing you to approach parenting challenges with a calm demeanor rather than a frazzled panic. Stress management becomes second nature as meditation trains your mind to remain steady amidst life's inevitable ups and downs. With regular practice, you develop an enhanced ability to respond thoughtfully rather than react impulsively. This shift in perspective can transform your interactions with your children, creating an atmosphere of patience and understanding.

Guided meditation isn't a one-size-fits-all practice; various styles are tailored to meet different needs. For fathers looking to unwind physically, body scan meditations are particularly effective. These sessions guide you through each part of your body, encouraging relaxation and release of tension. It's like giving yourself a mental massage without the cost of a spa day. On the other hand, loving-kindness meditations focus on fostering compassion for yourself and others. They encourage you to extend warmth and goodwill, helping to promote empathy and kindness in your daily interactions.

Meditation requires commitment but pays dividends in mental clarity and emotional resilience. Start by setting aside specific times each day for meditation. It doesn't have to be long—even ten minutes can make a difference. Morning meditations can set a positive tone for the day, while evening sessions help unwind and release accumulated tension. Creating a dedicated meditation space at home also reinforces this practice. This space doesn't need to be elaborate—just a quiet corner with minimal distractions where you can sit comfortably and focus inward. A few cushions or a favorite chair can transform any nook into your oasis.

Think of this practice as charging your mental batteries. The peace you promote spills over into other areas of life, enhancing overall well-being and happiness. The trick lies not in forcing meditation but in welcoming it as part of your routine—a gift you give yourself daily. As you become more attuned to the subtlety of meditation, you'll notice changes that extend beyond those few minutes of calmness. You might find yourself pausing before reacting, choosing empathy over anger, and embracing challenges with curiosity rather than dread. Guided meditation's beauty lies in its accessibility—it's available whenever you need it, no matter where or what you're doing. Whether seeking solace amid chaos or simply looking for moments of peace amidst life's busyness, this practice offers refuge and rejuvenation. Embrace guided meditation as an opportunity to connect with yourself on a deeper level—to explore the vast landscape within that often remains hidden beneath daily demands.

So next time life feels overwhelming, or stress threatens to consume you, remember this: guided meditation is your ally, ready to lead you toward inner calmness one breath at a time.

Breathing Techniques: Quick Calming Strategies

Imagine yourself standing amid a chaotic scene—children are squabbling violently over the TV remote control, creating a disharmony that echoes through the house. At the same time, the dog persistently barks back at a phantom squirrel outside the window as if holding a meaningful conversation. Your phone buzzes nonstop with work notifications that attract your attention like rapacious hands. At these moments, stress insidiously infiltrates your system, resembling an unwelcome guest at what was supposed to be a peaceful dinner party.

Amidst this chaos, breathing can transform into your secret weapon—an arsenal of calm against the army of stress. Indeed, something as innate and automatic as breathing holds extraordinary potential for provoking the tempest within. The breath is a direct bridge to your nervous system, capable of instantaneously transitioning your mental state from upheaval to tranquility with the power of a mere heartbeat. When slow, deliberate breaths are taken, they dispatch a soothing signal to your brain, commanding relaxation and successfully applying the symbolic brakes on the runaway stress response. This physiological marvel unfurls because deep breathing activates the parasympathetic nervous system, the division responsible for rest, digestion, and restoration, succeeding in calming your racing heart and comforting your frazzled nerves with effortless grace.

Let's delve into some beneficial breathing techniques that are easy to understand and straightforward to execute anytime, anywhere—no yoga mat or exotic setting required. The first technique is the 4-7-8 method, similar to a mental reset button, remarkable in its simplicity yet immense impact. Begin by inhaling through your nose for a slow count of four, hold this life-giving breath for seven deliberate counts, and exhale gently through your mouth for eight thoughtful counts. It's similar to offering your mind a comforting embrace, easing the tension that knots within and clearing the mental clutter that accumulates like dust in a seldom-used attic. Another treasure is box breathing, a technique often employed by seasoned Navy

SEALs for its unparalleled ability to foster focus and grounding. Envisioning a box, you inhale deliberately for four steady counts, hold your breath for four, exhale gracefully for four, and hold once more for four. This harmonious cycle is repeated until an unmistakable sense of grounding and centering envelops you. These techniques can be seen as portable stress-relief kits, perfectly compact and ready to deploy whenever life's chaos reaches such volumes that it threatens to consume your peace entirely.

Incorporating these breathwork exercises into your daily routine may be simpler than anticipated and can yield exponential benefits over time. Picture beginning your day with a few controlled rounds of deep breathing seamlessly woven into your morning ritual, perhaps during coffee brewing or the anticipation of the toaster popping. These brief moments of attentive breathing can set a serene tone for the day ahead, equipping you with a palpable sense of calm. As the day progresses and inevitably presents its challenges, utilize breath control techniques during stress-inducing encounters with your children. Should you find yourself teetering on the brink of losing patience amidst a tantrum or sibling dispute, pause briefly and breathe with intention. It is incredible how a few intentional breaths transform frustration into patience and understanding.

However, why keep this empowering tool solely to yourself? Sharing these techniques with your children gives them a lifetime of benefits and fortifies familial bonds. Leading a family breathing exercise session before bedtime could create a harmonious transition from the day's bustle to the restful embrace of the night. Encourage your children to practice these exercises to suppress school stress or before daunting exams. Imparting this knowledge—to use their breath as an anchor— endows them with invaluable skills, stimulating their ability to manage anxiety and embrace inner calm with confidence and poise.

Children, naturally eager sponges, absorb lessons most effectively through play and impression. Make breathing exercises a delightful journey by transforming them into a game, initiating a friendly competition to determine who can blow imaginary bubbles the most slowly, or rival the serene breathing of a gentle fire dragon. These playful interpretations convert learning into an enjoyable experience while sowing the seeds of critical life-long skills.

Breathing exercises transcend beyond mere stress relief; they are instrumental in calming space within ourselves to press pause and navigate life's complex demands with grace and remarkable resilience. They remind us that we retain dominion over our inner world amid swirling chaos. Embrace the opportunity to take a deep breath, allowing calmness to suffuse your being while exhaling any waiting tension or apprehension. Your breath, ever steadfast and reliable, remains a silent ally, ready to buoy you through any challenges you might confront. In those moments when life threatens to weigh you down with its overwhelming burdens and stress looms like an insatiable beast, ever poised to consume you whole, remember this core truth: within ourselves lies an immense power—the powerful simplicity inherent in the act of breathing—to rediscover calm amidst chaos and deliberately transform our responses from reactive to intentional, transforming an inharmonious reality into a symphony of serene intentionality.

Incorporating Mindfulness into Family Routines: Cultivating Calm and Connection

In the chaotic swirl of family life, searching for moments of peace is like searching for a needle in a haystack. The unending cycle of activities, obligations, and daily responsibilities can overwhelm even the most organized individuals. Yet, incorporating mindfulness into family routines can transform that metaphorical haystack into a fertile field of calm and togetherness. Imagine the family unit as a well-tuned orchestra, each member playing a unique instrument, contributing to a harmonious ensemble. Just as music requires dedicated practice and precise coordination, mindfulness practices also enhance family unity, fostering an emotional connection that resonates through every interaction. This collective mindfulness is like a balm, helping to reduce stress and anxiety and creating a shared sense of calm and stability that acts as an anchor during life's inevitable storms. Consider, for instance, a family gathering together for a mindful nature walk, where the typical focus on speed and destination shifts to relishing the journey. Instead of racing against time, each step becomes a cherished opportunity to connect with the environment and each other. The rustle of leaves in the gentle wind, the harmonious chirping of birds greeting the dawn, and even the satisfying crunch of gravel underfoot create a shared symphony of sounds that invites everyone into the present moment. Family yoga sessions, too, can weave mindfulness into movement, transforming every stretch and pose into a dance of conscious awareness and grace. Children can imagine themselves as playful animals, replicating the graceful stretch of a cat or the proud crane posture, while parents concurrently find balance and serenity in their practice.

Embracing Mindfulness as a Core Family Value

Creating a mindful family culture involves a commitment beyond scheduled activities; it's about embracing mindfulness as a core family value. Establishing meaningful rituals, such as a gratitude circle, can set the healing and appreciative tone needed. Gather around the dinner table or before bedtime, and take turns sharing something you are grateful for. This simple yet profound practice nurtures within everyone an attitude of appreciation and works to highlight the positive aspects of family life, which might otherwise go unnoticed. Additionally, encouraging open discussions about individual mindfulness experiences helps to reinforce its importance, fostering an atmosphere of understanding, empathy, and closeness.

Overcoming Hurdles to Mindfulness

Of course, introducing and maintaining family mindfulness practices isn't without its hurdles. Different ages and attention spans manifest unique challenges, requiring creativity and sometimes trial and error. Flexibility becomes the key to unlocking success. Adapt practices to suit each family member's needs—shorter activities for younger children who thrive on quick engagement and more extended sessions for teens or adults who may appreciate deeper dives into mindfulness. Consistency, the bedrock of successful implementation, can benefit from incorporating rewards or incentives. Perhaps it's offering an extra story at bedtime or allowing the children to lead and choose the next family activity. These seemingly small gestures can keep everyone motivated and engaged, eager to continue exploring the depths of mindfulness together.

The Ripple Effects of Mindfulness

Mindfulness practices contribute significantly to a more cohesive family unit by enhancing open communication and building unwavering trust. When each family member feels heard, seen, and valued, they're more likely to reciprocate those feelings within the group. This mutual respect creates a solid foundation, strengthening bonds and promoting emotional resilience. It empowers everyone to navigate life's inevitable challenges more easily, backed by the understanding and support cultivated through shared mindfulness.

Expanding the Benefits Beyond Family

Moreover, the benefits of mindfulness extend beyond the family gathering. They ripple outward, influencing the household dynamics and interactions within the wider community. As families become more mindful and emotionally connected, they naturally contribute to a kinder, more empathetic world. The transformative power of family mindfulness can inspire broader societal change, whether through active participation in community events or by simply sharing joyful and calm energy in everyday encounters.

In closing this expansive chapter on mindfulness and stress reduction, consider how these practices can further enhance your family's dynamics. Mindfulness isn't simply about isolated moments of solitude; it's about weaving connections through shared experiences that richly embellish everyday life. The beauty of mindfulness lies in its simplicity—no special equipment, elaborate preparation, or extensive training is needed, just a willingness to be present and open to life's moments.

In our next enlightening chapter, we'll explore how embracing vulnerability can deepen family relationships and foster greater emotional awareness. Until then, our collective wish is that your days may be filled with peace, presence, and playful moments of mindfulness that bring immeasurable joy to your family's ongoing journey together. May the calm be with you as you artfully navigate your shared lives' receding tide and flow.

REFLECTION JOURNAL PROMPTS

Take a deep breath....

These are just for you. There is no pressure to have the perfect answer—write what comes to mind.

"Mindful Moments: Finding Peace in Everyday Chaos":

1. What small practices help you stay centered and present during the most hectic parts of your day?
2. Can you recall a recent moment of calm or clarity, no matter how brief, and what made it meaningful to you?
3. How do you intentionally create opportunities for stillness or reflection in parenting and daily responsibilities?

"Breathing Techniques: Quick Calming Strategies":

1. How does your body typically respond when you feel overwhelmed or stressed? Have you noticed how your breathing changes in those moments?
2. What breathing techniques have you tried before, and how did they affect your mental or emotional state?
3. How might incorporating a short breathing practice into your daily routine shift your energy, mindset, or connection with others, especially your children?

"Incorporating Mindfulness into Family Routines: Cultivating Calm and Connection":

1. What daily routines in your home could be transformed into mindful moments, and how might that change the atmosphere for your family?
2. How do your children respond when you bring calm, present energy into shared activities like meals, bedtime, or transitions?
3. What simple mindfulness practices could you introduce to help your family reconnect during stressful or chaotic times?

"Overcoming Hurdles to Mindfulness":

1. What internal or external obstacles make it difficult to stay present, and how do you typically respond when those challenges arise?
2. When you've fallen out of mindfulness practice, what helps you return to it without judgment or pressure?
3. How might reframing mindfulness as a flexible, imperfect practice shift your expectations and increase consistency?

CHAPTER 9

MODELING EMOTIONAL AWARENESS

Leading by Example

Picture this: you're at the dinner table, and your child innocently asks whether you've ever feared the dark. It's a seemingly simple question, yet it opens a doorway into the complex world of emotions. Instead of tossing the question aside with a casual shrug, you lean in, meeting your child's gaze. "You know," you begin, allowing a reflective pause to emphasize the authenticity of your words, "I used to be terrified of the dark, too. It made me feel anxious and uneasy." This brief moment of vulnerability, a snippet of candid sharing, extends beyond mere storytelling; it serves as an installment in the ongoing course you're teaching your children about emotional awareness. You're setting a profound precedent by recognizing, naming, and sharing your emotions with them. In doing so, you communicate the unspoken lesson that feelings are natural and worthy of acknowledgment and exploration. Children often mirror what they see rather than what they're told. Therefore, when you acknowledge your emotions, you quietly encourage your child to do the same. This type of transparency doesn't merely assist them in navigating their inner emotional landscape; it emboldens them to do so with security and confidence.

Being emotionally aware doesn't imply you should transform into a continuous narration of your feelings as if you're producing a reality TV show centered on your life. It's more about finding those opportune moments throughout the day to pause, breathe, and reflect on what's happening inside your emotional sphere. You might say, "I'm feeling a tad overwhelmed today," then explain the day's events or stressors contributing to that feeling. By verbalizing the background for your feelings, you normalize the emotions and mold a pathway for your children to feel safe sharing theirs. Engaging in dialogues about emotional experiences with family members nurtures an environment brimming with trust and mutual understanding. It emboldens your children to express themselves freely, firmly reassured they won't be met with judgment or minimizing responses.

Carving out moments of self-reflection is integral to honing this skill. Set aside a designated time each day, perhaps in the evening or early morning, to engage in activities that promote mindfulness and emotional insights, like personal meditation. This isn't about achieving grand enlightenment but gaining clarity regarding the emotions meandering through your mind and the reasoning behind them. Meditation assists in calming the chaotic wanderings of the mind, thereby permitting you to tune into emotions that might otherwise slip by unnoticed. Another valuable practice is maintaining a journal. By logging your emotional recede and flow, you cultivate an awareness of what triggers specific emotional responses and how you react to them. This nurtures your emotional intelligence and highlights areas ripe for further development.

Sharing your emotional voyages with your children can have an indelible impact. Narrating stories where you've navigated emotional hurdles manifests resilience and adaptability. Through storytelling, we convey indispensable life lessons derived from emotional experiences. For instance, detailing a juncture where you were confronted with a tough decision, articulated with genuine feeling, can be an invaluable teaching moment. These narratives provide a context for understanding that emotions weave through the fabric of life; they are not daunting obstacles to evade but rather inextricable elements of human experience to understand and embrace.

To seamlessly integrate these practices into everyday life, establish routines that foster emotional awareness. Morning check-ins present an occasion to discuss anticipated emotional currents for the forthcoming day. Imagine it as setting an emotional compass, gauging where everyone stands before diving headfirst into the day's activities. Come evening, reflections provide opportunities to process emotions encountered throughout the day, creating rituals encouraging open dialogue and emotional exploration. These routines nurture a sense of connection and belonging within the familial structure.

You nurture emotional intelligence and fortify familial bonds by weaving these elements into your family's daily fabric. The journey towards fostering emotional awareness doesn't aim for perfection but celebrates consistent progress. Through modeling emotional awareness, practicing self-reflection, sharing personal journeys, and creating emotion-centered routines, you equip your children with invaluable tools, enabling them to navigate life's complexities both confidently and empathetically.

Reflection Exercise

Consider designating ten cherished minutes each evening for a heartfelt family reflection session. During this sacred time, invite each family member to share one distinct emotion they experienced that day and the circumstance or event that precipitated it. As everyone shares, lend an active, considerate ear to validate their feelings, consciously abstaining from judgment or interruption. Once everyone has had their turn, invite a discussion on any patterns or insights that might emerge from these revelations. This exercise doesn't just encourage open communication; it weaves an environment where emotions are not stifled or diminished but celebrated and embraced, solidifying the importance of transparent and empathetic communication within the family unit.

Encouraging Empathy in Your Kids: The Art of Understanding

Imagine your little one witnessed a sibling getting upset over a broken toy. Instead of brushing it off, you seize the moment. "How do you think your sister feels?" you ask gently. This simple question introduces empathy, a crucial life skill. Empathy is about stepping into someone else's shoes and understanding their feelings. For children, this can start with relatable scenarios. Picture books with empathetic characters can be great tools. Stories about animals helping each other or friends resolving conflicts can illustrate empathy. Discussing these tales helps children see emotions from different perspectives. It turns storytime into a lesson on understanding and kindness.

Role-playing is another fantastic way to nurture empathy. Imagine setting up a little theater in your living room where your kids can act out various roles. Maybe today, your child plays the part of someone feeling left out while you or a sibling takes on the role of the friend offering comfort. This exercise not only makes empathy tangible but also fun. It shows kids how to express concern and offer support. Volunteering as a family is another hands-on approach. Whether serving meals at a shelter or helping neighbors with yard work, these activities show children the importance of caring for others. They learn that small acts of kindness can have a significant impact.

Helping children recognize and validate emotions is key to calming empathy. Please encourage them to express their feelings about what happened during the day. You might say, "I noticed you seemed quiet after school. Do you want to talk about what happened?" This invites them to share openly. When they do, practice active listening. Reflect on their words to show understanding. If they say, "I was sad when my friend didn't play with me," respond with, "It sounds like that hurt your feelings." This validation reassures them that their emotions are legitimate, not something to hide or dismiss. Promoting kindness and compassion starts at home and in everyday interactions. Create a kindness jar where children can jot down acts of kindness they perform, like helping a sibling or sharing a toy, and place them in the jar. Once it's full, celebrate as a family. Maybe have a kindness pizza night or an extra story before bed. Recognizing and rewarding these actions reinforces the value of empathy and encourages them to continue being compassionate. Celebrating empathy and kindness within the family creates a positive feedback loop, inspiring kids to keep spreading kindness wherever they go.

Encouraging Open Communication: Creating Safe Spaces

For children to feel comfortable sharing their feelings, they need a safe environment where their thoughts are respected and valued. Establish non-judgmental spaces at home where discussions flow freely without fear of criticism or dismissal.

Set family rules that emphasize respectful listening, ensuring everyone has a chance to speak and be heard.

Incorporate regular family meetings into your routine to facilitate open dialogue. Use this time to discuss everyone's feelings and experiences from the week. Open-ended questions like "What made you smile this week?" invite more than just yes or no answers, encouraging deeper conversations.

Active listening and validation are crucial in these discussions. Reflect on what your child says to show that you understand and acknowledge their emotions without dismissing them. If they express frustration over a school project, say, "I hear you're feeling overwhelmed by this project." This affirmation helps them feel seen and supported.

Encourage problem-solving discussions by brainstorming solutions together when emotional challenges arise. If your child is upset about a conflict with a friend, work together to develop strategies for resolution. Ask questions like, "What do you think would help improve things?" This empowers them to take charge of their emotions and find constructive solutions.

Creating safe spaces for open communication does more than help children express themselves; it lays the groundwork for lifelong healthy relationships built on trust and understanding.

Building Emotional Vocabulary: Giving Kids the Words They Need

Imagine, if you will, a common yet significant moment in a child's life: they have misplaced their favorite toy. This cherished companion has accompanied them on countless adventures. They stand before you, their little face scrunching to communicate the swirling emotions inside. Most will say they're "mad," but such a word barely scratches the surface of their feelings. The truth is that an entire spectrum of emotions is hidden beneath that single declaration of anger. It might be a cocktail of frustration over having lost sight of the toy, disappointment over not being more careful, or even a touch of sadness for not having it by their side. Thus, providing a child with a rich emotional vocabulary is similar to giving them a painter's palette with an array of vibrant colors, empowering them to express themselves more precisely and vividly. When children can accurately identify and articulate their emotions, they develop a better capacity for emotional management, enhancing their ability to communicate effectively with others around them. Language and emotional insight are interwoven intricately; without the appropriate verbal tools, emotions remain as complex, tangled knots, much like an indecipherable ball of yarn, complex to unravel and far more challenging to manage.

Consider for a moment the implications of a limited vocabulary. This scenario can significantly hinder a child's ability to express emotions, often inadvertently leading to frustration and a profound misunderstanding. When children lack the necessary words to articulate their internal states, it resembles the challenge of describing a complex flavor without the appropriate gastronomic lexicon. Such barriers in communication often manifest externally, resulting in behavioral phenomena such as acting out or withdrawing, driven by the inability to convey their rich inner tape. By intentionally expanding their emotional vocabularies, we bestow upon them the empowering ability to express thoughts and feelings with clarity. This newfound articulation minimizes misunderstandings and nurtures and fosters stronger, healthier relationships.

Introducing new and varied emotional words into a child's speech repertoire need not be intimidating. A practical starting point could be using flashcards adorned with emotional words, each accompanied by vivid, corresponding facial expressions. It transforms learning into an engaging game, where each card becomes a portal to a deeper, more nuanced understanding of emotions. Integrate the use of these cards during relaxed moments, seamlessly weaving their introduction into everyday family activities. Moreover, make a conscious effort to incorporate these novel words into everyday dialogues. Instead of an overused "happy," opt for the more nuanced "elated" when describing the joy of winning a game. This not only embellishes vocabulary but also assists children in discerning the subtle distinctions between various emotional states.

Storytime: A Gateway to Emotional Insight

Stories and media serve as a fertile educational landscape for emotional exploration. When reading a book or engaging in a movie experience, periodically pause the narrative flow to delve into the characters' emotional nuances and complexities. Gently pose questions such as, "How do you think he felt when that event occurred?" or "What might you have done if you were in her place?" Such discussions act as thought-provoking prompts, urging children to venture into emotions from multiple angles, broadening their empathetic horizons, and helping them see the multifaceted world through the diverse eyes of others. It transcends the task of identifying feelings, encompassing an understanding of motivations and potential consequences. This deliberate process transforms media consumption from a passive experience into an active, interactive learning endeavor.

Visual Learning: Bringing Emotions to Life

Visual aids hold tremendous potential as pedagogical instruments, capable of solidifying learning concepts tangibly. Constructing an "emotion word wall" at home can be a joyful and educational venture. Designate a special wall or bulletin board area for this ongoing project. Encourage a collaborative family effort, with children regularly contributing by adding fresh emotion words and using them creatively within sentences. Turn it into a fun family ritual—each week, introduce a new emotion-related term, dissect its various connotations, and wrap up with a creative session where your children illustrate what each emotional state looks or feels like, transforming it into a lively art project that breathes life into these abstract concepts. This visual yet tactile representation is a constant cognitive reminder, reinforcing the vocabulary they have diligently acquired over time.

Through these meaningful and multifaceted practices, we facilitate opening up channels of communication that might otherwise remain obstructed by the limitations of language. By equipping our children with the expressive words they need, we provide them with navigational tools essential for confidently journeying through their emotional landscape. It transcends mere vocabulary building; it fundamentally establishes lasting connections—bridges between feelings and comprehension. Through this enlightening process, we ensure that our children genuinely feel heard and understood in every dimension of their existence, fostering a healthy emotional foundation upon which they can thrive.

The Magic of Active Listening

Active listening transcends merely filtering sounds or hearing words; it demands a full engagement that genuinely understands the essence of what's being shared. Imagine your child returning home, heavy-hearted, from a day at school where they felt left out during recess. In such scenarios, capturing the heart of what they're saying and then reflecting it to them can be immensely validating. By doing so, you're affirming the value of their expression and demonstrating that you are truly present with them. Consider saying, "It sounds like it was tough when your friends played without you." This potent yet straightforward reflection acknowledges their experience and signals a beacon of empathy. In practicing this, a powerful message is imparted—that it's perfectly alright to feel the myriad emotions life stirs within us. Such acknowledgments cultivate a nurturing space where emotions are normalized and respected as natural facets of being human. Encouraging problem-solving discussions adds another dimension to cultivating emotional intelligence. When emotional or other challenges arise, involving your child in brainstorming solutions fosters a sense of ownership and empowerment. Perhaps they're plagued with anxiety over an impending math test. Posing a question such as, "What do you think would help you feel more prepared?" opens the door to collaborative thinking. This approach embeds within them the confidence to take ownership of their emotions and seek constructive pathways forward. Encouraging children to devise solutions nurtures independence and critical thinking skills that bloom mightily as they transition into adulthood. Wrapping up this insightful exploration into creating safe spaces for open communication, remember that this journey is an ongoing endeavor. It calls for patience, enduring understanding, and unwavering consistency. You're already laying splendid groundwork by consciously establishing environments devoid of judgment, fostering open discussions, mastering the art of active listening, and promoting problem-solving dialogue. These practices cultivate robust emotional foundations in your children, fortifying them with invaluable skills that will serve them well in the present moment and continue to support and enrich their lives into the future.

In the upcoming chapter, get ready to dive into the beautiful art of creating a legacy of love—a heartfelt discussion on how these essential elements play a vital role in boosting your and your children's emotional well-being. Stay tuned and prepare yourself for some uplifting insights on fostering balance and nurturing harmony in the incredible journey of family dynamics!

REFLECTION JOURNAL PROMPTS

Take a deep breath....

These are just for you. There is no pressure to have the perfect answer—write what comes to mind.

"Encouraging Empathy in Your Kids: The Art of Understanding":

1. How do you model empathy in your everyday interactions, and what do you notice about how your children respond or reflect that behavior?

2. Can you recall a time your child showed genuine empathy? What did it reveal about their understanding of others' emotions?

3. What strategies have you found effective in helping your kids see things from someone else's perspective, especially during conflicts or misunderstandings?

"Encouraging Open Communication: Creating Safe Spaces":

1. What steps have you taken to show your children that they can speak honestly without fear of judgment or punishment?

2. How do you respond when your child shares something difficult or uncomfortable, and how does that shape their trust in you?

3. What rituals or routines could help make open communication a natural part of your family's daily life?

"Building Emotional Vocabulary: Giving Kids the Words They Need":

1. How do you help your child name and express their emotions, and what challenges have you faced?
2. What emotional words or concepts do you wish you had learned earlier in life, and how are you introducing them to your children now?
3. How can everyday moments—like playtime, conflict, or storytelling—be used to expand your child's emotional vocabulary?

"Visual Learning: Bringing Emotions to Life":

1. How have you used visual tools, like emotion charts, drawings, or stories, to help your child recognize and understand their feelings?
2. What role does creativity (like art, facial expressions, or role-play) play in how your child expresses or makes sense of emotions?
3. How might incorporating more visual or hands-on methods improve emotional communication in your home?

"The Magic of Active Listening":

1. When was the last time you felt truly heard? What made that moment impactful, and how can you offer the same to your child?

2. Do you notice habits or distractions that prevent you from fully listening, and how do you work to overcome them?

3. How has practicing active listening changed how your child opens up to you or expresses themselves?

CHAPTER 10

CREATING A LEGACY OF LOVE

They Deserve a Whole Parent—And So Do I

Imagine your life as a jigsaw puzzle. Pieces scattered everywhere, some flipped upside down, others missing that pesky corner. Now, picture yourself with all those pieces snugly in place. That's what it means to be a whole parent. It's about being fully present, offering balance and stability, like a sturdy ship navigating the sometimes-turbulent waters of family life. Wholeness isn't just about ticking boxes—it's about creating a nourishing environment where you and your children thrive, integrating emotional, physical, and mental well-being into your parenting toolbox. When you embrace the entirety of your being, you create an atmosphere where your kids feel safe and cherished.

Self-care, dear friend, is more than just a trendy term thrown around by wellness gurus; it's the cornerstone of feeling whole and fulfilled. Imagine it as that all-important oxygen mask on an airplane—you need to tend to your own needs before you can help others. Make it a point to carve out regular personal time for your favorite hobbies or to unwind, enjoying those activities that lift your spirits. These cherished moments are key to keeping everything in harmony, whether painting, nurturing your garden, or delighting in a peaceful cup of coffee. Let mindfulness be your reliable companion, guiding you through stress and keeping you grounded amid the wonderful chaos of parenting.

Embodying wholeness serves as a powerful example for your children. When they see you practicing healthy habits and setting boundaries, they learn the importance of self-care and emotional intelligence. Share your personal growth journeys with them—talk about the challenges you've faced and the lessons you've learned along the way. Doing so teaches them that growth is a continuous process, not a destination. They begin to understand that being human means embracing both strengths and vulnerabilities.

Reflection Exercise

Take a moment to reflect on how you currently balance personal and family needs. Identify areas where adjustments could be made to ensure everyone in the family has time for self-care and individual growth. Consider discussing these reflections with your family to collaboratively create a schedule supporting personal and collective well-being.

By embracing being a whole parent, you craft a legacy of love that extends beyond immediate relationships. It's about creating a family culture where everyone feels valued and empowered to grow. You're not just raising children; you're nurturing future adults who will carry forward the lessons of love and resilience you've instilled in them.

This Is How It Ends With Me (But Starts With Them)

Imagine standing at a crossroads, where the path behind is littered with the weight of old habits and inherited patterns. It's easy to feel overwhelmed by the past, that pesky shadow that clings persistently. But there's power in recognizing those negative cycles, the whispers of past generations echoing through your actions. By identifying these inherited behaviors, you're choosing to break the chains and start fresh with your children. This isn't about erasing history but filtering the best parts and leaving the rest behind. It's about crafting a new story where love, understanding, and resilience take center stage.

Self-reflection becomes your compass in this transformative process, guiding you through the rough patches. Think of it as a spotlight illuminating the areas that need attention. Through journaling about family history and personal growth, you gain insights into the patterns that have shaped your parenting style. You see the threads connecting past and present, unraveling those that no longer serve you while weaving new ones that align with your values. This introspection isn't just a solitary activity; it's a conversation with your past, an opportunity to understand its influence and make conscious choices moving forward.

Change is a powerful catalyst for empowerment. As you implement positive changes in your life, you'll notice a ripple effect that extends to your children. Celebrating personal and family growth milestones becomes an integral part of this journey. These celebrations don't have to be grand gestures; small victories sometimes hold the most significance. Share stories of transformation with your children, highlighting moments when you chose a different path or embraced a new perspective. These narratives become their inheritance, a testament to the strength and determination it takes to forge a new legacy.

Crafting a new family narrative involves more than words; it's about creating traditions and rituals that embody healthy values. Documenting family stories that reflect positive changes serves as both a record and a reminder of how far you've come. It could be a family scrapbook with photos, captions, and mementos from shared experiences. Or it's creating new family traditions like Sunday brunches where everyone shares their highs and lows from the week. These rituals instill a sense of belonging and continuity, grounding your family in a shared vision for the future.

As you build this narrative together, remember that you're not just writing a story for today but crafting one for generations to come. The values you instill now will echo through time, shaping the future in ways you can only imagine. It's about setting a foundation where your children feel empowered to carry forward these lessons, adapting them to their lives and circumstances. Your family's story becomes a living entity, evolving with each generation while remaining rooted in love, resilience, and growth.

Through conscious efforts and intentional choices, you're not just ending old cycles but creating space for new beginnings. This is how it ends with you, but it starts with them.

Crafting a Legacy of Love: Your Family's Future

Imagine sitting around the dining table, surrounded by the laughter and chatter of your loved ones, as you lay down the foundation for a legacy of love that will span generations. What does this mean for you and your family? It starts with defining core values and principles that guide every decision and every action. Think of these values as the compass that keeps your family on course, no matter how stormy the seas might get. Establish long-term goals aligning with these values—fostering kindness, promoting education, or ensuring everyone feels heard and cherished. It's about painting a picture of what you want your family to stand for today and far into the future. Involving everyone in this process makes it a shared endeavor. Host family discussions where each member can voice their thoughts and dreams. Encourage even the youngest to contribute ideas—kids often surprise us with their wisdom and creativity! These discussions reinforce family bonds and ensure everyone feels invested in the legacy you're building. Allowing each member a say creates a collective vision reflecting your family's diverse strengths and aspirations.

Sustaining this legacy through generations requires more than talk. It's about teaching your children the stories and values that shaped your family history. Share tales of ancestors who embodied these values, illustrating how they navigated challenges and celebrated victories. This helps children understand their roots and instills pride in their heritage. Please encourage them to carry these lessons and pass them on to their children one day. It's a chain reaction, where each link strengthens the next, ensuring the legacy of love endures.

To preserve this legacy tangibly, consider creating a family time capsule filled with meaningful items that capture your family's essence. It could include letters, photographs, or objects that represent significant milestones. Compiling a family history book with stories and lessons serves as a record and a guide for future generations. These tangible reminders help keep the legacy alive, offering future family members a window into their past and a roadmap for their journeys.

Celebrating small wins along the way is just as important as achieving big goals. Recognize daily acts of kindness and effort, acknowledging each family member's progress. Create a culture where progress is valued and celebrated—this can be as simple as sharing successes at the dinner table or creating a visual progress chart to track achievements like learning new skills or completing projects. By fostering an environment that appreciates growth, you cultivate motivation and resilience within your family. Embracing a growth mindset means viewing setbacks not as failures but as opportunities to learn and improve. Discuss lessons learned from challenges during family meetings, reinforcing that growth is a continuous process.

Lifelong learning becomes integral to this legacy, fueling personal development for parents and children. Engage in educational activities together, sparking curiosity and exploration in everyday life. Whether attending workshops or reading books on new topics, these experiences expand horizons and foster a love for learning. Share your learning journey with your children, discussing insights gained from personal development activities and encouraging them to explore their interests. This commitment to growth ensures that your family's legacy remains vibrant and evolving.

Celebrating Small Wins: Recognizing Growth

Imagine a world where every small victory is met with a high-five, a pat on the back, or even a little family jig in the living room. Celebrating those small wins isn't just about the momentary joy it brings; it's about fostering motivation and growth. When you acknowledge daily acts of kindness and effort, you fuel the fire of self-confidence in your kids—and yourself. It's like finding loose change in your pocket; small, but gratifying. Each recognition plant is a seed that nurtures resilience and a can-do attitude. It's about ensuring everyone knows their contributions matter and that they're seen, heard, and appreciated.

Creating a culture of celebration within your family is like setting up a perpetual festival of positivity. Establishing a family ritual for sharing successes turns the dinner table into a stage for applause, where everyone gets their moment in the spotlight, no matter how small the achievement. Think about creating a visual progress chart that hangs proudly on the fridge or a wall. It's not just a chart; it's a living testament to everyone's efforts. Watching those sticky stars or smiley faces accumulate is a visual reminder of progress and dedication. This visual celebration of success fosters an environment where growth is anticipated and eagerly pursued.

Encouraging personal and family growth is similar to nurturing a garden. Every bit of praise and encouragement you offer for personal milestones acts as nourishment, helping each family member to flourish. Reflecting on family achievements during gatherings turns what could be mundane chats into meaningful conversations that underscore collective progress. These reflections serve as both a moment to look back and a springboard to leap forward. Celebrating individual triumphs alongside family victories creates an atmosphere where everyone feels supported and motivated to continue reaching for their personal best.

The fear of failure can be a stubborn thorn that pricks at our potential, but it needn't be so. By shifting perspective and viewing setbacks as stepping stones rather than stumbling blocks, you empower your family with resilience and resolve. Encourage a growth mindset in response to challenges, transforming moments of adversity into opportunities ripe for learning. Discussing lessons learned from failures during family meetings normalizes the experience and strengthens the bond of mutual support and understanding. Turning failure into a shared learning experience fosters unity and builds resilience.

As you create this vibrant tapestry of celebration and growth, remember that every small win is a stitch in the fabric of your family's legacy. These victories, whether as simple as learning to tie shoelaces or as significant as achieving personal goals, contribute to a culture that values progress over perfection. By recognizing growth in all its forms, you lay down pathways for future success, encouraging everyone in your family to keep moving forward with confidence and joy.

The Journey Continues: Embracing Lifelong Learning

Picture this: a family gathered around the kitchen table, books and papers spread out, laughter mingling with the scent of freshly brewed coffee. That's the magic of engaging in educational activities as a family. It's about more than just learning new facts; it's about fostering curiosity and exploration in everyday life. When you turn a trip to the local museum into a treasure hunt or transform a simple nature walk into a biology lesson, you ignite a spark of curiosity in your children. This enthusiasm for learning becomes infectious, creating an environment where questions are welcomed and discoveries are celebrated.

Opportunities for personal development abound if you know where to look. Consider attending workshops or seminars on parenting and personal growth. These events offer fresh perspectives and practical tools that can revitalize your approach to both parenting and life. Imagine the insights gained from diving into books that challenge your thinking or introduce new interests. Whether you're exploring mindfulness techniques or the latest in child psychology, these resources open doors to growth and understanding. They provide a way to expand your knowledge while setting an example for your children about the value of lifelong learning.

Creating a home that encourages learning and curiosity requires intention. Set up a family library with diverse reading materials for all ages and interests. This collection becomes a treasure trove of knowledge just waiting to be explored. Encourage open discussions about new ideas and concepts during family meals or car rides. These conversations broaden horizons and strengthen bonds as everyone shares their thoughts and perspectives. By nurturing this environment, you cultivate a home where learning is as natural as breathing. Sharing your learning journey with your children can be incredibly rewarding. Discuss the new insights you've gained from personal development activities, whether it's a newfound appreciation for meditation or tips on improving communication skills. Children who see that learning doesn't end with school are inspired to pursue their interests and passions. Encourage them to share their experiences, too—whether it's excitement over mastering a new skill or curiosity about a topic they've recently discovered. This knowledge exchange fosters a culture of mutual respect and collaboration within the family.

Interactive Element: Family Learning Adventure

Plan a "Family Learning Adventure" day, during which each family member chooses an activity or topic they'd like to explore together. This could be anything from visiting an art gallery to trying out a cooking class or even taking an online course in astronomy. Rotate the responsibility of planning these adventures, allowing everyone to share their passions and interests with the rest of the family.

Embracing lifelong learning isn't just about acquiring knowledge; it's about cultivating a mindset that values growth and exploration. It's a commitment to staying curious, open-minded, and engaged with the world around us. When learning is an integral part of your family's life, you enrich your experiences and lay the groundwork for your children to thrive in an ever-changing world.

Gratitude and Growth: Honoring the Path Traversed

Picture this: a quiet moment at the end of a hectic day, pen in hand, jotting down thoughts in a gratitude journal. It's a simple act that can transform how we view our lives. Practicing gratitude isn't just about saying "thank you" for the big stuff; it's about acknowledging the small blessings that often go unnoticed. Keeping a gratitude journal helps you reflect on these daily gifts, fostering a sense of appreciation for personal and family Growth. Each entry becomes a reminder of progress and positivity, nurturing an outlook that values ordinary and extraordinary moments.

Sharing gratitude during family meals can turn dinnertime into a celebration of connection. Imagine each person taking a moment to express what they're thankful for that day, creating an atmosphere of warmth and unity. This practice encourages everyone to recognize the beauty in their lives, strengthening bonds and fostering empathy. It's not just about the words; it's about the feeling that lingers, the understanding that we're all in this together, navigating life's ups and downs with gratitude as our guide.

The journey's challenges and triumphs form a tapestry woven from struggles and victories. Encourage yourself to honor these by reflecting on significant milestones and the lessons gathered along the way. Celebrating resilience in adversity builds a foundation of strength, reminding you of your capacity to overcome. It's about looking back with pride at how far you've come and acknowledging the hurdles you've overcome with grit and determination. This reflection isn't just a solo act—share these stories with your family, highlighting the resilience that defines you.

Incorporating gratitude into family life can be as simple as establishing a gratitude ritual or tradition. It could be a weekly family meeting where everyone shares what they're thankful for or a gratitude jar where notes of thanks are collected. Encouraging children to express gratitude regularly instills a lifelong habit of appreciation. This practice nurtures empathy and compassion, teaching them to see the world through a lens of kindness and understanding.

Growth is an ongoing process, not a destination. Embrace it as an ever-evolving journey filled with possibilities. View life as a series of learning opportunities, where each experience contributes to your development. Remain adaptable and open to change, knowing that growth often emerges from unexpected places. Encourage a mindset that sees challenges as stepping stones, not stumbling blocks. By staying receptive to new experiences, you promote an environment where growth thrives.

As you weave gratitude and growth into your family's fabric, you create a legacy of love that transcends generations. Each moment of appreciation adds depth to your story, reminding you of the beauty found in everyday life. It's about honoring the path traversed while eagerly anticipating the road ahead, knowing that you're building a legacy defined by love, resilience, and gratitude with every step.

A Vision for the Future: Parenting with Purpose

Picture this: a family dinner where everyone shares their dreams and aspirations, united by a shared vision. Purposeful parenting is about creating a family environment that aligns with your deepest values and goals. Begin by setting clear intentions for your parenting practices, like making a blueprint for the future you want to build together. Think about what truly matters to you and your family. Is it kindness, resilience, or perhaps a love for learning? Identifying long-term family objectives helps keep everyone on the same path, providing direction and focus even on the most chaotic days.

Aligning daily actions with your family's overarching purpose is crucial. Getting swept up in the daily grind is easy, but keeping your actions intentional can make all the difference. Every decision, from how you spend your time to how you communicate, should reflect your family's core values. Reflecting on daily actions becomes a habit; think of it like a mental check-in at the end of each day. Did today's choices support our family's goals? If not, what can we tweak tomorrow? This ongoing reflection ensures that your journey stays true to its course, allowing you to adjust and adapt as needed.

Inspiring your children with purpose is one of the greatest gifts you can offer. By sharing personal stories of purpose-driven decisions, you show them that living with intention is not just an abstract idea but a tangible way of life. Please encourage them to explore their purposes and passions through hobbies, volunteering, or simply asking questions about the world around them. When kids see their parents living purposefully, it plants a seed that grows into a lifelong quest for meaning and fulfillment. You become their role model, teaching them that purpose isn't something you find; it's something you create.

Creating a legacy of purpose is about more than just setting goals—it's about impacting future generations. Please encourage your children to carry forward the legacy of purposeful living by involving them in decision-making and goal-setting from a young age. Document your family's purpose and vision in a way that they can refer back to throughout their lives. This could be a family mission statement framed in your home or a journal where everyone contributes ideas and reflections. These tangible reminders serve as guideposts, ensuring that the legacy you build today continues to inspire tomorrow.

As we wrap up this chapter on parenting with purpose, remember that the choices you make today shape your family's present and future. Through intentional living, you create a space where everyone thrives, supported by shared values and mutual understanding.

REFLECTION JOURNAL PROMPTS

Take a deep breath....

These are just for you. There is no pressure to have the perfect answer—write what comes to mind.

"This Is How It Ends With Me (But Starts With Them)":

1. What generational patterns or behaviors have you consciously chosen to end, and what has that process looked like for you?

2. How do you hope your healing or intentional choices will shape your children's future and the kind of parents they might become?

3. What legacy of love, safety, or emotional truth are you committed to building that begins with your decision to break the cycle?

"Crafting a Legacy of Love: Your Family's Future":

1. What values, traditions, or emotional truths do you want your children to carry into adulthood and pass down to future generations?

2. How are your daily actions—big or small—contributing to the legacy you hope to leave behind?

3. What would a loving, connected, and emotionally healthy family legacy look like to you, and what steps are you taking to create it now?

"Celebrating Small Wins: Recognizing Growth":

1. What recent moment made you feel proud of yourself or your growth as a parent or person, no matter how small?

2. How do you acknowledge progress in your family, and how might celebrating small wins encourage continued emotional growth?

3. How can you shift your focus from perfection to progress and celebrate the everyday efforts that often go unnoticed?

"The Journey Continues: Embracing Lifelong Learning":

1. What recent experience, challenge, or insight has taught you something new about yourself or your approach to parenting?

2. How do you stay open to growth, even when it's uncomfortable or old habits try to creep back in?

3. What kind of learner are you becoming as a parent, and how do you model curiosity and humility for your children?

"A Vision for the Future: Parenting with Purpose":

1. What kind of relationship do you hope to have with your children, 5, 10, or 20 years from now, and what are you doing today to nurture that vision?

2. Which values or life lessons do you most want to pass on, and how do they guide your daily parenting choices?

3. How does parenting with intention shape the legacy you're building for your children and yourself?

.

CONCLUSION

Here we are, at the end of this journey together. We've navigated the winding, sometimes bumpy roads of fatherhood, and hopefully, you've found some new paths that lead to a more fulfilling and nurturing environment for your family. If there's one thing I hope you take away, the transformation from parenting through pain to creating a loving, resilient family is not just possible; it's within your reach.

Throughout this book, we've delved into the heart of emotional awareness, the cornerstone of effective parenting. Understanding and managing your emotional landscape can feel like untangling a ball of yarn in a drawer for years. But once you start, you realize the knots aren't as tight as they seemed. When you know your emotions, you can respond rather than react; that difference can change everything. Communication has been a thread running through each chapter. Active listening and empathetic responses aren't just buzzwords; they're tools that build bridges between hearts. Imagine hearing what your child is saying, not just the words but the emotions beneath them. When you respond with empathy, you show them that their feelings matter. These skills are the glue that strengthens family bonds, creating a foundation of trust and understanding.

Breaking generational cycles is no small feat. It's like deciding to rewrite the script of a play that's been performed the same way for decades. But it's possible, and it starts with conscious choices. By recognizing patterns that don't serve us, we can choose to parent differently. We can create a new narrative where love and understanding lead the way, setting a healthier stage for our children and their future families.

Emotional healing and personal growth have been central to our journey. These aren't one-time achievements; they're ongoing processes that enrich your life and your children's. The healing benefits are profound, whether through mindfulness practices, reflection, or seeking support. You're mending old wounds and cultivating a garden where new, beautiful things can grow.

As you've seen, mindfulness is a powerful tool for reducing stress and enhancing presence. It's about finding quiet moments amid the chaos of daily life where you can breathe and reconnect with what truly matters. When you practice mindfulness, you're not just calming your mind; you're modeling a way of being that your children can learn from and rival.

Encouraging emotional intelligence in your children is one of the greatest gifts you can give them. By helping them understand and articulate their emotions, you're equipping them with the tools they need for life. Empathy, understanding, and open communication will serve them well in every relationship they build.

As we conclude, I want to leave you with a vision—a legacy of love that extends beyond your lifetime. Imagine the ripple effect of your intentional parenting, influencing generations to come. Your efforts today are laying the groundwork for a future where love, empathy, and understanding are the norm.

But remember, this journey doesn't end here. Personal growth and conscious parenting are lifelong commitments. Keep learning, keep growing, and keep striving to be the best version of yourself for your family. The road may twist and turn, but you're making a difference with each step.

I am grateful to have shared this journey with you. Thank you for your openness and willingness to explore new ways of being. Know that you have my support as you apply these lessons in your own life. Together, let's continue to create families where love and understanding thrive. You're not alone on this path; the best is yet.

ABOUT THE AUTHOR

As a single father, I am navigating the rewarding yet challenging journey of co-parenting two foster children with my ex-wife. Being dedicated to fostering, I truly understand the mental and physical hurdles that come with caring for children who have faced unique struggles. It's a balancing act, managing these responsibilities while also experiencing moments of growth, resilience, and joy along the way.

Though life after divorce is challenging, I'm committed to providing stability and love for my children. I recognise that even in difficult circumstances, co-parenting is a shared journey. With a passion for helping others, I share my experiences to provide support and insight to those facing similar struggles in fostering and parenting.

I aim to be real and honest. I never claim to be perfect, but I always strive to create a positive, understanding environment for my children.

With gratitude and support,

D. McMahon

SOURCE MATERIAL

1. Powerful Possibilities of the Transformational Parenting. (2025). *www.jaiinstituteforparenting.com*. Retrieved from https://www.jaiinstituteforparenting.com/peaceful-parenting-method

2. Parental Anxiety: Knowing If You Have It and Finding Relief. (2025). *www.healthline.com*. Retrieved from https://www.healthline.com/health/parenting/parental-anxiety

3. 5 Serious Long-Term Effects of Yelling At Your Kids. (2025). *www.healthline.com*. Retrieved from https://www.healthline.com/health/parenting/effects-of-yelling-at-kids

4. How to Unlearn Toxic Relationship Patterns - HealingWorks. (2025). *www.healingworks.co*. Retrieved from https://www.healingworks.co/blog/breaking-generational-curses-how-to-unlearn-toxic-relationship-patterns

5. Book Review – Raising an Emotionally Intelligent Child. (2025). *psychiatryresource.com*. Retrieved from https://psychiatryresource.com/bookreviews/raising-emotionally-intelligent-child-review

6. Developing empathy in families.pdf. (2025). *nurturingparenting.com*. Retrieved from https://www.nurturingparenting.com/images/cmsfiles/developing_empathy_in_families.pdf

7. Emotional triggers and relationship issues in therapy. (2025). *sunshinecitycounseling.com*. Retrieved from https://www.sunshinecitycounseling.com/blog/emotional-triggers-and-relationship-issues-in-therapy

8. . (2025). *positivepsychology.com*. Retrieved from https://positivepsychology.com/building-self-awareness-activities/

9. Active listening.html. (2025). *cdc.gov*. Retrieved from https://www.cdc.gov/parenting-toddlers/communication/active-listening.html

10. . (2025). *hopskipdrive.com*. Retrieved from https://www.hopskipdrive.com/blog/empathic-listening-skills-that-build-trust-with-children/#:~:text=CPI%20defines%20empathic%20listening%20as,time%20and%20effort%20to%20learn

11. . (2025). *breakthesilencedv.org*. Retrieved from https://breakthesilencedv.org/why-fathers-should-be-vulnerable-with-their-children-a-story-of-healing-and-unconditional-love/

12. Fathers role breaking emotional unavailability. (2025). *fherehab.com*. Retrieved from https://fherehab.com/learning/fathers-role-breaking-emotional-unavailability

13. What is a dysfunctional family 5194681. (2025). *verywellmind.com*. Retrieved from https://www.verywellmind.com/what-is-a-dysfunctional-family-5194681

14. . (2025). *positivepsychology.com*. Retrieved from https://positivepsychology.com/conscious-parenting/

15. . (2025). *growingself.com*. Retrieved from https://www.growingself.com/breaking-generational-cycles/

16. Narrative therapy for trauma. (2025). *healthline.com*. Retrieved from https://www.healthline.com/health/mental-health/narrative-therapy-for-trauma

17. How to achieve work life balance as a father. (2025). *daduniversity.com*. Retrieved from https://www.daduniversity.com/blog/how-to-achieve-work-life-balance-as-a-father

18. . (2025). *gabb.com*. Retrieved from https://gabb.com/blog/digital-detox/

19. . (2025). *stdavidscenter.org*. Retrieved from https://www.stdavidscenter.org/article/quality-time/

20. . (2025). *fatheringtogether.org*. Retrieved from https://fatheringtogether.org/fatherhood-support-groups/

21. . (2025). *pmc.ncbi.nlm.nih.gov*. Retrieved from https://pmc.ncbi.nlm.nih.gov/articles/PMC11120519/

22. . (2025). *pmc.ncbi.nlm.nih.gov*. Retrieved from https://pmc.ncbi.nlm.nih.gov/articles/PMC7331354/#:~:text=Research%20has%20shown%20that%20parental%20empathy%20is%20positively%20associated,attachment%20security%20and%20emotional%20openness.&text=Parents%20with%20strong%20empathy%20provide,comfort%20when%20experiencing%20emotional%20distress.

23. . (2025). *choosingtherapy.com*. Retrieved from https://www.choosingtherapy.com/vulnerability-hangover/

24. . (2025). *rockandart.org*. Retrieved from https://www.rockandart.org/modern-fatherhood-in-the-uk-parenting-practices/

25. . (2025). *positivepsychology.com*. Retrieved from https://positivepsychology.com/inner-child-healing/

26. . (2025). *positivepsychology.com*. Retrieved from https://positivepsychology.com/resilience-activities-exercises/

27. . (2025). *positivepsychology.com*. Retrieved from https://positivepsychology.com/benefits-of-journaling/

28. . (2025). *dmh.lacounty.gov*. Retrieved from https://dmh.lacounty.gov/mental-health-resources/fathers-support-hub/

29. 3 powerful mindfulness techniques for busy dads stay calm stay present 101609f3a382. (2025). *medium.com*. Retrieved from https://medium.com/@mindfulfather/3-powerful-mindfulness-techniques-for-busy-dads-stay-calm-stay-present-101609f3a382

30. Art 20045858. (2025). *mayoclinic.org*. Retrieved from https://www.mayoclinic.org/tests-procedures/meditation/in-depth/meditation/art-20045858

31. He.stress management doing breathing exercises.uz2255. (2025). *healthy.kaiserpermanente.org*. Retrieved from https://healthy.kaiserpermanente.org/health-wellness/health-

encyclopedia/he.stress-management-doing-breathing-exercises.uz2255

32. Five mindfulness strategies to help your family cope with anxiety. (2025). *hopkinsmedicine.org*. Retrieved from https://www.hopkinsmedicine.org/health/conditions-and-diseases/anxiety-disorders/five-mindfulness-strategies-to-help-your-family-cope-with-anxiety

33. Emotional intelligence first five years life. (2025). *child-encyclopedia.com*. Retrieved from https://www.child-encyclopedia.com/emotions/according-experts/emotional-intelligence-first-five-years-life

34. Icd.2397. (2025). *onlinelibrary.wiley.com*. Retrieved from https://onlinelibrary.wiley.com/doi/full/10.1002/icd.2397

35. . (2025). *positivepsychology.com*. Retrieved from https://positivepsychology.com/kindness-activities-empathy-worksheets/

36. . (2025). *centerforresilientchildren.org*. Retrieved from https://centerforresilientchildren.org/emotional-vocabulary/

37. . (2025). *gottman.com*. Retrieved from https://www.gottman.com/blog/emotional-intelligence-creates-loving-supportive-parenting/

38. . (2025). *hollyhillhospital.com*. Retrieved from https://hollyhillhospital.com/blog/understanding-generational-trauma-breaking-the-cycle/

39. . (2025). *thelincolncenter.com*. Retrieved from https://thelincolncenter.com/everyday-mindful-practices-to-strengthen-family-connections/

40. . (2025). *hospicewaterloo.ca*. Retrieved from
https://www.hospicewaterloo.ca/legacy-activities/